This book is dedicated to the one I speak to first when
I begin a story, who inspires me, blesses me, and carries
me page by page to the end—my Father in Heaven.

ISBN 13: 978-1-4621-4078-7

Published by Sweetwater Books, an imprint of Cedar Fort, Inc.
2373 W. 700 S., Springville, UT 84663
Distributed by Cedar Fort, Inc., www.cedarfort.com

Library of Congress Control Number: 2021950599

Cover design by Shawnda T. Craig
Cover design © 2022 Cedar Fort, Inc.
Edited and typeset by Valene Wood

Printed in the United States of America

10 9 8 7 6 5 4 3 2 1

Printed on acid-free paper

Murder has a Ball

Shannon Symonds

SWEETWATER BOOKS
An imprint of Cedar Fort, Inc.
Springville, Utah

Other Books by This Author

Safe House
Finding Hope
Murder Takes a Selfie
Murder Makes a Vlog

Contents

1. Falling Leaves & Friends 1

2. When the Committee Should Be Committed 7

3. Storm on the Horizon 16

4. Who's on Your Dance Card? 26

5. The Refreshment Committee... 39

6. The Decorating Committee.. 47

7. The Fairy Grandmother 54

8. May I Have This Dance? 57

9. Is This the Last Dance?... 76

10. The Costumes We Wear 82

11. Pumpkins & Mice 105

12. Paying the Price of the Ticket... 112

13. The Clean-Up Committee 118

14. The Cast and Crew 136

15. I Object! 145

16. The Subcommittee..151

17. Behind the Mask... 162

18. The After Party.. 171

19. Zombie with Two Left Feet 174

20. The Curtain Call...181

About the Author 185

Chapter One

Falling Leaves & Friends

Esther's stepfather, Papa J, drove his Jeep Cherokee through a pile of autumn leaves and laughed loudly. Esther held on to the bar on the dash and couldn't help but smile. She looked at her best friend, Sophie, in the back seat, rolled her eyes, and they both started laughing.

"Look at that pile!" He veered the Jeep toward a mountain of leaves on the shoulder of the gravel road.

"Look out! There's a . . ." Esther braced herself.

The Jeep fell into a ditch hidden by the leaves. Papa J expertly swung the Jeep out and back onto the road, laughing like a wild man.

"Nice off-roading." Sophie adjusted her round black glasses and smoothed her long black hair. "I can't wait until we can drive ourselves in the van."

"I love this time of year. You kids are doing a good job restoring the VW van. Not too much longer and it'll be ready for a road trip." He turned the Jeep off the gravel road and onto the main highway toward the high school. While pulling into the carpool lane with the other parents and busses delivering kids, he switched on the radio.

Music played while they idled and slowly crept closer to the two-story high school. Trees dropped their leaves on the muddy lawn in the roundabout. In the early morning hours, warm light poured out of the small-paned windows.

"This is River Peace with KLAM, your Coho County station, for when you want to stay in the know, and get your Zen on. It's seven fifteen on October 17, and it's all seventies in the sevens. Call in your requests. In the news today: It's official. The filming of the movie, *Blessed Be*, based on our local Madison Merriweather's book, has officially been postponed as the director is resting comfortably in prison. Family Friendly films are now looking for a director who doesn't kill people. And to the cat who put liquid dish soap in the town square fountain—well done. The bubbles are blowing by the sea." The radio cranked out *Lola* by The Kinks. Papa J started singing along.

The girls locked eyes. Esther's eyebrows rose, and the giggles started again. Without shame, Papa J smiled at her and kept on singing.

Oceanside High School was built sometime in the late 1800s. It had a gothic flavor. Its gray slabs of stone and windows were decorated with carvings. Sophie and Esther had decided long ago that it needed gargoyles.

As they pulled up to the high school entrance, Esther gathered the books that had slid out of her backpack on the wild ride and stuffed them back in.

"Thanks for not killing us," Sophie said.

Smiling, Esther reached over and gave Papa J a quick hug. "You're the best."

A gust of frigid wind caught the car door when she opened it and blew her brown hair into her eyes. Pulling her hoodie over her head, she wriggled into her backpack and dashed for the door behind Sophie. Rain spattered onto the broad sidewalk and concrete steps leading to the main hall. The wind sent the last of the autumn leaves skittering across the sidewalk.

With Sophie's help, Esther pushed the big doors open. Pulling off her hood, Esther headed for their first-period class, Library Science. It wasn't actually a class. Both girls had more than enough credits in order to graduate and were only taking advanced placement courses. The librarian, Ms. Priest, had arranged for them to work in the library for the balance of the day as student aids. It was a win-win for the girls who loved the vintage library, with its black oak walls and shelves. Esther especially loved the stone fireplace and leather couches. It was a cozy place to study.

"Esther! Sophie!" Paisley Stuart waved at them from ahead in the river of humanity. She held the hand of Esther's uncle, Nephi, and pulled him upstream until they reached the girls. Paisley's shoulder-length blonde hair was down and straight. It rested just above her fisherman's sweater.

"Did she dress Nephi?" Sophie asked.

Esther realized they were wearing matching white cable-knit sweaters. They looked like they should be in a sports ad for fishing.

Esther loved her uncle. He resembled her. He had the same brown, wavy hair and muddy green eyes with gold flecks.

Falling into step with the girls, Paisley let go of Nephi's hand. She walked backward, hands on her backpack straps, facing the girls. She said, "Hey, I have a huge favor. You know I'm on the student leadership committee with Nephi and we're working with the boosters? Well, two members of my committee for the homecoming ball and Halloween haunted house have mono. So, I signed you up." Grinning sheepishly, she raised her eyebrows. "Well?"

Jackson Green, six-feet-four-inches of solid concrete and auto grease, leaned against his locker, intensely watching Paisley walking backward toward him. His long, greasy black hair hung over his brown eyes.

Esther saw the crash coming and put her hands up. She tried to warn Paisley, but it all happened too fast.

At the same time, Jackson Green stepped away from his locker and purposely stood like a human wall. Paisley collided with his solid form. Jackson grabbed Paisley's backpack before she could fall to the ground and lifted her back to her feet.

Stepping between Paisley and Jackson, Nephi pushed Jackson. "Watch it! You did that on purpose."

Jackson shoved Nephi back. He flew and hit a nearby locker. Jackson's mouth fell open. His eyes were wide as he ran toward Nephi.

"Sorry, man," Jackson said. "Sorry!"

Still sitting on the ground, Nephi took his foot and landed it squarely in Jackson's stomach. The kick pushed him back until he tripped over Paisley's feet and fell backwards on the floor.

"Jackson!" Mr. Conner Kelly, the new principal, bellowed.

"How does he do that?" Sophie whispered to Esther. "It's like he senses broken rules in the universe and appears like a dark lord."

"Sophie!" Esther shook her head. "Don't get us into trouble."

"Jackson. Nephi. My office."

Fists clenched, eyes narrowed, Jackson leaped to his feet and turned away from the principal. Students got out of his way as he silently strode past Esther and down the hall to the school entrance. He opened the steel doors so hard they slammed against the outside walls. He walked right out of the school, and the doors slammed behind him.

Esther, Sophie, and Paisley watched with their mouths hanging open.

"Whoa," Esther said. "I would never do that."

"No duh. You wouldn't jaywalk if your hair was on fire." Sophie gave Esther a friendly push and chuckled.

Paisley helped Nephi to his feet. "Are you all right, baby?"

Narrowing his eyes, Nephi pressed his lips in a straight line and looked at Mr. Kelly.

"Baby? Baby?" Baxter Jones, or Bubba, as everyone at school called him, started mimicking Paisley. "Baby?" Taller than Jackson by two inches and twice as smelly, Bubba laughed loudly. Esther had never seen Jackson without Bubba. They were always in trouble together. His gray eyes closed under his dirty blond hair. His smile showed his yellow teeth.

"I should pull that ring out of your eyebrow," Sophie said.

"If you could reach it, shorty," Bubba chuckled and smirked.

Mr. Kelly said, "What's going on? Baxter, while I appreciate your loyalty to Jackson, he can take care of himself. Now everyone, get to class. You too, Sophie."

Nephi just shook his head and shrugged as he passed the girls on the way to the principal's office.

The bell rang loudly, and the students began emptying the halls like rats scurrying to their holes. Parker said goodbye and headed to his class. Esther, Sophie, and Paisley opened the library door and slipped inside.

"What just happened?" Esther asked Paisley. "Did Jackson Green do that to you on purpose?"

Paisley rolled her eyes and shrugged. She took off her backpack and let it drop to the floor. "Nephi should know I can take care of myself. He didn't need to kick Jackson or get into a fight. The last thing I need is another committee member to be absent from school."

Ms. Priest, the librarian, emerged from her office to join the conversation. She had sleek black hair like Sophie's that fell past her shoulders. She wasn't much taller than Esther, but she was very thin and always wore heels, making her appear tall and stately. Today, however, she wore jeans, clogs, and an oversized black sweater to guard against the chill in the library.

Using her library voice, Ms. Priest said, "Sorry, I couldn't help but overhear. I have been suspecting that Jackson likes you, Paisley, but doesn't quite know what to do about it. It kind of reminds me of when I was in elementary school. If someone liked you, they pulled your pigtail." While she spoke, Ms. Priest turned on the light switches closest to the front counter of the library. "Not saying I approve of his method."

"Well, this isn't kindergarten, and that wasn't cool. He purposely tried to make Paisley fall." Sophie tucked her backpack under the counter and hung her coat on the rack by Ms. Priest's office door. Esther kept her hoodie on and put her backpack away. She took the keys out of the coffee cup on the countertop and unlocked the cash drawer. The library was now open for business.

"Wait. Look at this," Paisley said. "He must have pushed this note in my backpack when I was falling over."

Paisley unfolded the paper and smoothed it out on the library counter. All four of them gathered for a closer look. It was a piece of lined paper torn out of the kind of notebook that leaves a million tiny pieces along one edge. On the lined paper was a perfect likeness of Paisley's face, drawn in pencil. It wasn't signed.

"I rest my case." Ms. Priest grinned with satisfaction, wrinkled her nose, and winked at the girls before she went back into her office to work.

"Well, what kind of ding dong knocks you down to give you a gift like this?" Sophie asked.

"A shy one." Esther knew exactly how Jackson felt. For years she'd been anxious and awkward around people she didn't know. Only recently had she been brave enough to make new friends.

"He may be shy, but he gives me the shivers." Paisley shook all over and brushed her arms off, as if she were making Jackson go away.

"He's kind of pathetic," Esther said. "I mean, maybe I am wrong, but I feel sorry for him. His dad owns the tow truck, right?"

"Yeah, so?" Sophie tipped her head, and her brows knit together.

"I just think he doesn't have anyone but his dad who obviously doesn't take care of him. His clothes are always torn up and sometimes covered in paint. They live in the junky trailer park. It's just . . ." Shrugging, Esther chewed her lip, thinking. "I feel sorry for him."

"You'd feel sorry for a serial killer," Sophie laughed.

Paisley's cell phone chimed. "It's a text from Nephi. They're both suspended for a day for fighting. Grandma Mable is coming to get him. Great. That's one less person on the dance committee. Right when I need help." She sighed heavily. "I have to get to biology. Will you guys help me? I really need it."

Esther nodded. "Sure. Tell us what we need to do."

"Speak for yourself," Sophie said. Then she smiled. "Kidding! Of course we'll help. It will be great. But what do we have to do? Seriously?"

"It's easy. Trust me. Okay? The boosters and dance committee meet here, in the library, after school. Join us and I'll go over everything then."

Chapter Two

When the Committee
Should Be Committed

Esther and Sophie pushed opened the ornate library doors leading to the parking lot and stepped out into the weather. The doors closed, and they heard the lock click into place. A cold gust of wind shook the leaves on the giant rhododendrons that surrounded the stone steps. Even though it was only a few minutes past two, it already felt like evening. Steel gray clouds mixed with heavy black rain clouds rolled and wrestled across the sky. The sea air blew across the river, through the wetland grass and Esther's hair. It made Esther smile. She had a strange fondness for the salty, fishy smell that wafted in from the ocean.

In a synchronistic cold weather ritual, Esther and Sophie pulled their hoods over their heads and zipped up their hoodies. With their backpacks in place, they silently crossed the parking lot and walked along the gravel road toward Esther's home by the sea.

"We have an hour to go home, grab food, and beg for a ride back. Think we'll make it?" Esther said.

"I am sure it's okay if we're a little late. I'm hangry."

"Nephi texted. He said Mr. Kelly is making him and Jackson work on the dance committee as penance for fighting. It's that, or he gets a standard four-day suspension for fighting. This way they're only suspended for one day. They're supposed to learn to work together. I wonder if Mr. Kelly gave them the option because Paisley begged for committee members?" Esther chuckled.

Sophie shook her head. "That sounds like a recipe for an interesting group. Hey. I was wondering if Parker asked you to the Halloween Homecoming dance?"

"We haven't really talked about it. We've been busy working on the van, and school. It hasn't come up."

"He should do something like Jake Tucker did for Rainbow. He took her an ice cream cake with the invitation inside the cake. You're going to go, aren't you?"

"You know, I never dated before Parker. I can't believe I'm saying this, but I am just so happy to hang out with him, I hadn't really thought about it."

Sophie stopped. She shook her head at Esther. "You have to invest in a relationship. I was reading *Today's Teen Magazine* . . ."

Esther rolled her eyes and held a hand up, laughing. "Don't quote to me from that rag. Seriously." She couldn't contain a giggle. She smiled like a Cheshire cat and said, "Nine hundred fun and flirty ways to get a guy. Be bikini ready." They dissolved in laughter.

"I was doing research," Sophie said.

"You read one?" Esther started walking again, side by side with Sophie.

"I was kind of hoping to get a date for homecoming, besides you and Nephi this time." Sophie shrugged.

"Did you have anyone in mind? I am sure someone will ask you. Personally, I think it's more fun to go with a big group."

"Easy for you to say. You've got a date who's not only hot and rich, but he's fun and smart too."

Esther knew she was right. Parker was unusual.

A black BMW pulled up alongside the girls. The tinted passenger window rolled down. It was Paisley and her twin, Esther's boyfriend, Parker.

"Did you forget?" Paisley said. "The Homecoming Committee meeting at the library starts soon."

Esther beamed. She couldn't help it. Parker was smiling at her from the driver's side, and she smiled back with her entire face. Her pulse always jumped when she saw his blue eyes, blond hair, and handsome face.

"Get in!" Parker hit the locks. Sophie and Esther took off their backpacks and climbed in the back.

"We remembered. We're just starving. I could eat a vegan horse." Sophie took off her hood and buckled her seat belt. "Can we get something to eat first?"

"You're always hungry, Sophie Eats." Parker chuckled as he used her nickname, signaled, and turned onto the empty small town road. "Actually, we're hungry too. We're running to the food carts to get some tacos before the meeting. Do you think we should get some for Nephi and Bridget?"

"That's sweet. I agree. I'll pay for Nephi and Bridget's tacos. I have some cash." Esther started fishing in the front pocket of her pack.

"Don't be silly," Paisley said. "We'll get a big taco box for everyone and I'll buy."

The smell of the box of tacos sitting in Esther's lap was making her stomach growl. She turned her attention to Parker's easy smile, dimples, and chiseled face. He winked at her, knowing she couldn't wink back. It was a skill she had never been able to master. She fluttered her eyelashes, and he smiled his smile, the kind of smile that created laugh lines from a lifetime of finding the good and the humor in everything and everyone.

She'd only dated Parker for five months, but during those months, her life had changed. And she realized she'd changed in a good way. The Stuart twins treated each other and their friends like family. Their generosity and kindness were contagious.

Parker pulled into the lot next to the library, got out, and opened Esther's door. After unbuckling, she and Sophie carried in cardboard boxes filled with tacos and warm tater tots covered with foil.

Paisley ran up the stone steps ahead of them, her expensive Frye boots making noise on the stairs. She banged on the doors.

"Ms. Priest! Hello?"

Ms. Priest appeared on the other side of the small-paned windows in the heavy steel doors and unlocked them.

"Get in here. It's starting to hail. I didn't expect you this soon." Ms. Priest talked loudly over a strong wind gust. The doors slammed and hail began pelting the windows and ceiling so loudly they all stopped and looked back at the parking lot. Quickly it was covered in white ice. Hail bounced on the steps and grounds like piles of popcorn.

"Good timing." Principal Kelly appeared again, as if by magic.

Esther looked down to see what kind of shoes he wore. *How does he do that? No sound at all*, she thought.

"Hello, Principal Kelly. I was just making tea and a snack. I don't have much to offer." Ms. Priest motioned towards a tray of cookies and a steaming pot of tea on the table in front of the unlit fireplace. She had pushed more chairs into the circle.

Mr. Kelly smiled at Ms. Priest. "That looks like a lovely offer," he said and wiggled his eyebrows. Ms. Priest's normally alabaster cheeks turned blood red, and a little frown line appeared on her flawless face. Principal Kelly stepped closer to Ms. Priest and Esther's stomach knotted. *I know that look. That's the same look Papa J gave Mom before he proposed.*

"Employers shouldn't pressure employees," Sophie whispered and gave Esther a knowing look, eyebrows raised over her round glasses.

"Shush." Esther looked to see if Principal Kelly had heard Sophie. "Ms. Priest can handle him. I have complete faith in her."

"Let's eat. I'm starving," Sophie said.

Paisley added the tacos to the tea table.

Esther watched Principal Kelly stand uncomfortably close to Ms. Priest. He sniffed and smiled at Ms. Priest, like a wolf inviting a little girl in a red cape to dinner at Grandma's house. Esther couldn't look away.

"The principal is really in her space, and she obviously doesn't like it," Esther whispered.

While everyone moved in for food, Sophie leaned closer to Esther. They stared at Ms. Priest's rigid body language and Principal Kelly's continued invasion of her personal space.

"That's disgusting and very unprofessional," Sophie said. She shook her head. "That's all we need. The principal hanging out in the library telling more dad jokes and making poor Ms. Priest crazy."

"Ms. Priest," Esther called. "Would you like a taco?" She stepped in between Ms. Priest and Principal Kelly.

"Thank you, Esther."

Principal Kelly looked at Esther and left the library.

Ms. Priest sighed, loud and long.

Esther finished her taco and was contemplating the tater tots when Mr. Kelly returned and got on the subject of plumbing the fireplace with a gas line.

"Sorry I'm late, lovelies." Madison Merriweather, now a best-selling author of two books, *Blessed Be* and *Solstice,* swept dramatically into the room, removing her black rain cloak.

Her daughter, Bridget, passed her mother. "Did you save me a taco?" She began foraging.

The door opened again, blowing a gust of cold air into the already chilly library. Nephi, Papa J, and Esther's mother, Grace, came in, surprising Esther.

"Esther. Did you eat?" her mom asked. She shook the rain off her rain jacket and hung it up.

"Paisley bought us a box of tacos. They were great," Esther said.

"Pass me five tacos." Nephi plopped his tall frame onto the antique sofa.

"You ate at home." Papa J shook his head and sat behind Nephi in a chair. Her mother pulled up a chair next to him.

"What kind of tea did you make?" Grace asked.

"Cinnamon chai, no caffeine," Ms. Priest said.

"Oh! May I have some?" Esther's mom got up and poured herself a cup. She settled in, still shivering as she held the warm mug in her hands, the steam rising.

"Grace, you're shaking. Would you like my cape?" Madison stood. Even though Grace shook her head no, Madison wrapped the cape around Grace's lean frame. Engulfed by the cape, Esther's mother smiled at Madison, while steam from her tea seeped out of the cape.

"I am going to give this school a gift. I am going to buy you all the gas plumbing or whatever you need for the fireplace. The library may look cozy, but it's drafty and wet." Madison nodded at Principal Kelly and Esther had no doubt they would have a working fireplace in a few days. No expense would be spared.

The door opened again and this time the wind blew a few tacos onto the floor. Nevaeh Rose, and her mother, Angelica Rose, fell through the door. It took both of them to push it closed against the whistling wind.

"The fun has finally arrived," Nevaeh announced, holding both her hands in the air. She smiled with her whole face, from her tiny perky nose to her bright eyes. Wearing sheepskin-lined boots, and her favorite green hoodie, which matched her green eyes, and yoga pants that hugged her ample hips, she looked all Oregon Coast. She shook out her frizzy brown ringlets, getting water on her mother.

Angelica Rose held up her hands to stop the shower, but it was too late. She frowned at Nevaeh and sighed. Her dark hair was slicked back in a tight knot at the nape of her neck. Water dripped from her false eyelashes, and she used her manicured nails to wipe drops from the tip of her nose, leaving exposed skin where makeup had been. Removing a name-brand hooded raincoat, she adjusted a tight, but expensive-looking black jogging suit. Finally, she looked for a place to hang her coat. She settled on the back of a chair a little way away from the group.

Paisley stood up. "Thanks for joining us, I am so pleased . . ." Paisley was interrupted when the door opened and three more people joined the group.

Esther wasn't surprised to see Aiden Van Doren come in with the Stuarts. He was a familiar face at high school events. She studied him while Paisley hugged her parents, and Parker gave up his seat on the couch to his mom.

Esther motioned to Parker and scooted closer to the arm of the couch. He squeezed in between her and Sophie, putting his arm around her. She snuggled into his warmth and the smell of clean laundry.

Aiden Van Doren wasn't much older than Ms. Priest, maybe a little over thirty. It was hard to tell with his spray tan and athletic build. He was a graduate of Oceanside High, who, on the coattails of his now-deceased father, had made good. He owned a large auto dealership that drew customers from four counties, both local spas, and a gym.

He must spend a lot of time at the gym, Esther thought.

Sophie elbowed Esther. "What's up with Van Doren and Priest?" Pointing with her eyes and motioning with her head, Sophie made a wide-eyed look of surprise and then cocked one eyebrow. Esther followed her gaze. Ms. Priest had moved to sit next to Aiden Van Doren, and they were looking into each other's eyes, laughing and talking quietly.

Esther nodded to Sophie, who made another face, which Esther completely understood. She knew what her friend was trying to say. *Crepes. Look who likes each other.*

Esther whispered, "He seems nice."

Paisley stood in front of the fireplace, so everyone was facing her.

"I would like to thank my friends and family for jumping in and helping when several of our committee members contracted the kissing disease." She made a coy face and wiggled her eyebrows. Light laughter rolled through the gathering. "I'd like to ask you all to stay healthy and avoid kissing, as we have our work cut out for us. I want to start by giving everyone an update."

"You're so organized. My inner geek is happy." Sophie accepted a stack of paper from Paisley, took one, and passed the rest on to Esther.

After passing the stack along, Esther examined the long list of steps to prepare for the dance. The back of the paper had a list of necessary supplies.

"To recap from our last meeting and for our new folks, the dance will be called the Homecoming Masquerade Ball. Because our homecoming football game falls so close to Halloween this year, we went with the theme of Masquerade, patterned after *The Phantom of the Opera*. The song *Masquerade* will be our opening dance. The tickets will be made with popsicle sticks and paper masks." She held up a sample. "Aiden Van Doren has graciously volunteered to bring in several movie projectors to project old black and white movies of dances, balls, and even the movie we are using as inspiration for our theme. The dance will be held in our beloved library."

Paisley took a breath and looked around the room. "Ms. Rose?"

Esther looked at Nevaeh's mom and realized her mouth was drawn down into a frown. Even Botox, if she had it, wasn't going to stop her brows from drawing together in the center. She followed her gaze across the room to Mr. Van Doren and Ms. Priest, who were smiling at Paisley, but obviously leaning as close to each other as possible.

"Ms. Rose?" Paisley said louder.

Ms. Rose seemed to wake up. She made a syrupy smile and looked at Paisley, but didn't say anything.

Paisley cleared her throat and continued. "I want to thank you for generously sponsoring the dance. I've decided we should have a candy bar, or a large spread of candy, candied apples, sweet popcorn, and treats for the dance. We will also be making vats of homemade root beer. Since you own the Sweet Treat Shops in Necanicum and Cabbott's Cove, would you be willing to get us an estimate of the cost of refreshments in the next few days?"

"I'll do better than that." Angelica stood looking at Van Doren and waited until she had everyone's attention. "I'll donate all the refreshments, if you kids don't mind coming to the shop and helping me make the candy. We'll make taffy, fudge, and candied apples at our candy store. It's what I do best. It will take four to five hours and at least five of you to do the work. I'll also donate gourmet root beer. What do you think?"

Everyone clapped. Paisley gave the room one of her beautiful white smiles.

"That's wonderful! I will send around a blank sheet. Everyone that wants the dance to be a success should sign up to help make the candy." Paisley winked at Esther, Parker, and Sophie, and smiled at Nephi.

"You don't have to ask me twice to make candy, if I get to eat the rejects." Sophie took the paper and signed them all up.

After Angelica sat down, Mr. Van Doren raised his hand. Paisley nodded at him.

"Ms. Priest and I would like to work with River Peace on the music. I'll also donate a fog machine and Cynnomon will bring twinkle or fairy lights for the ceiling."

Then it happened. Ms. Priest and Aiden held hands, and Esther heard a sharp intake of breath from Angelica Rose's direction. Angelica's daughter, Nevaeh, stood up and left the room.

"Excuse me," Angelica said. She followed Nevaeh out.

Ms. Priest's face became bright red. Esther couldn't remember ever seeing her so embarrassed.

Aiden Van Doren stood up. "I'll be right back." He followed the Roses out into the dark school hallway.

As soon as Aiden left, Principal Kelly stood. He crossed the room and took Aiden's seat next to Ms. Priest. A shiver ran up Esther's spine when he put his arm around Ms. Priest, leaned in and said something Esther couldn't hear. Ms. Priest pulled away and folded her arms.

Paisley continued, but Esther couldn't focus on her. She was too busy listening to the raised voices in the hallway. "I'm sorry I didn't . . . I never promised . . ." For a minute, she heard Nevaeh's voice. Then she thought she heard Mr. Van Doren say, "Grow up."

Rain began falling in heavy drops on the metal roof, riding the wind and slapping against the glass panes. The deluge drowned out the heated discussion in the hall and the library for a moment. Old-fashioned streetlamps came on in the parking lot as the sun set. Esther got up and turned on the lamps in the sitting area.

She looked at Ms. Priest, whose mouth was still open. Her eyes were locked on the door. When Aiden Van Doren came back into the room, he looked like the dark storm clouds that had rolled in that afternoon. Principal Kelly was still in his seat. He stood behind Ms. Priest. It was a long time before the Roses joined them again.

Ms. Rose came in with her arm around Nevaeh, whose eyes were red-ringed. She had a clump of the little toilet paper squares, the kind found in school bathrooms, clutched in her hand, but she didn't make a sound and there were no tears.

The west doors to the library opened one more time. Rain blew in and left a pattern on the hardwood floor. Ironpot, still in his Necanicum Police Department uniform, stood silhouetted in the last light of the day. Holding the door for Mrs. Ironpot, he stepped to the side and sucked in his ample girth.

Mrs. Ironpot smiled as she passed him and took off the hood to her rain jacket. Her pink cheeks matched her pink sweatsuit and large pink coat.

"Sorry, we're late. We had to pick up Jackson. He's helping decorate for the dance. Did we miss anything?" Karen Ironpot asked.

Jackson stepped into the room and dripped on the floor. Watching the puddle collect, his dark hair hung in his eyes, no coat, a soaked t-shirt, and his hands stuffed into the pocket of his wet jean pockets.

Chapter Three

Storm on the Horizon

Esther and Sophie helped Ms. Priest shut down the library after the meeting. Esther's mother, Grace, and Papa J moved the circle of chairs away from the fireplace. They carried them to the various study tables lit by ancient lamps and scattered around the large room. Ms. Priest carried her teapot to the teacher's lounge to wash it. Esther and Sophie helped her by gathering the mugs.

The hall was dark, but they all knew the way to the teacher's lounge. Ms. Priest opened the door and turned on the light. At the same time, a flash of lightning lit the room up and the power went out. Thunder rolled around the building. They looked up as if they could see it through the ceiling.

"I think I'll wash these first thing in the morning." Ms. Priest filled the old-fashioned china teapot with soapy water. Sophie turned on the flashlight on her cell.

Ms. Priest smiled weakly in the dim light. "Girls, after what happened tonight, I am hoping I can confide in you. We've known each other for a while now."

Esther nodded. "It's been a few great years."

"I've had exceptional students come through the libraries I've worked in. Not many were as brilliant as you two are, but still, they find a special place in my heart. Your resilience and kindness toward others makes you exceptional to me. You two are kindred library lovers. But as a teacher . . . well . . ." Her words trailed off. She chewed her lip while vigorously washing the inside of the teapot.

Esther wondered where Ms. Priest's speech was going. "You aren't quitting, are you?"

Ms. Priest laughed her musical laugh. The sound that always infected whatever room she was in.

"No! Well, not unless I'm fired after tonight. I feel like we have been through enough together that I want to give you girls an explanation."

She doesn't have to. But I am dying to know what's going on. Esther looked at Sophie, who met her gaze.

"You see . . ." Ms. Priest hesitated. She looked down, turned on her cell phone flashlight and began washing the teapot she had planned to leave for the morning. "We . . . I . . ." She stopped and looked at the girls. "As teachers, and as a librarian, I'm supposed to set an example at school and in the community. When Aiden—Mr. Van Doren— asked me out, I thought we decided to keep it quiet. I don't like drama and wanted to wait until we were sure we'd continue dating."

Sophie's chin pulled in, and she put her free hand on her hip. "You're entitled to a life, Ms. Priest. We would never judge you. And if the school made you sign a contract that you would be an old maid librarian, I am going to start a petition. That's archaic. Work is work, and your personal life is your life." Obviously feeling protective of Ms. Priest, Sophie's words came out quickly.

"Yes, but, I prefer not to mix my personal life with my work life." Another flash of lightning lit up Ms. Priest's tired face. "Anyway. I would appreciate it if we could not make tonight's events a matter of school gossip. Not just for my sake."

"Do you mind if I ask how it impacts the Roses? I worry about Nevaeh," Esther asked.

In the light of the phone, Ms. Priest took a deep breath and let it out slowly. She bit her lip and looked at Esther with sad eyes. "I love the fact that you care so much about others, Esther. It is one of your finest qualities. Mr. Van Doren and Nevaeh's mom were dating. He really cares about Nevaeh, but things didn't work out." She shrugged.

"No kidding, things weren't working. We all heard it wasn't working, loud and clear tonight," Sophie said.

Ms. Priest dried the teapot and put it in a cupboard that was labeled *library*. "We better get you two home. The morning will come quickly. I know you may talk to family and friends about tonight. I guess I just hope it doesn't go out over social media. Thank you for listening. Whatever you decide to do, I'll understand."

"I've been social-media bullied before," Esther said. "We get it. Honestly, I'm more worried about Principal Kelly."

Ms. Priest stopped moving for a moment and seemed far away. After a few seconds she shook her head, smiled brilliantly at Esther, and said, "That can wait until tomorrow. I'm exhausted. People love to talk." She grinned, but her eyes betrayed her concern.

"Sheesh. Esther had her life all over social media when her father thought he should have custody and tried to kidnap her. We get it. Totally. People can be so mean when they can snipe at you across the net. Your personal life is safe with us." Sophie held up her hand. "Scout's honor."

"Why do you always say that? No scout troop would have us," Esther laughed.

"Pinky swear?" Sophie held out a hooked pinky finger.

Ms. Priest gathered both girls in a quick hug. "Sorry. Breaking the hug rule, too. Thank you." She stepped back and held the door to the faculty lounge open. "Now, let's get out of here before I break another rule."

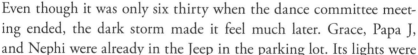

Even though it was only six thirty when the dance committee meeting ended, the dark storm made it feel much later. Grace, Papa J, and Nephi were already in the Jeep in the parking lot. Its lights were on and it was idling when Esther, Sophie, and Ms. Priest closed and locked the library door.

Ms. Priest dashed for her car. Esther and Sophie piled into the back seat of Papa J's car.

"Stop kissing." Esther buckled her belt. Her mother just laughed. "You newlyweds are so gross."

"Well, little miss smarty pants. Do you want to drive us home?" Grace was grinning at Esther when the dome light went off.

"Esther? Drive?" Nephi laughed. "Maybe we should all walk." Lightning flashed and thunder rolled across the sky.

"Not tonight. There's lightning. We never have lightning in Necanicum. It's a sign. We should go home and drink hot chocolate," Esther said.

"Dinner first." Her mom reached over and held Esther's stepdad, Joe Hart's hand. Her mother leaned over and kissed his cheek.

"Gross. It was worth a try. Weren't the tacos enough?" Esther smiled at Sophie.

"Toy food? Never," Nephi grumbled.

"I have to get home, practice my violin, and study so I make valedictorian before you," Sophie said.

"Then I have to have to study too, because I am going to own that title."

"Dream on, E. Dream on."

The power was back on and the streetlamps were lit when Papa J dropped Sophie at her house and parked in front of their large Victorian home. The surf was so rough Esther could hear it as she ran through the rain to the door.

After a quick dinner of leftovers, Esther's seven-year-old sister, Mary, read her school assignment to Esther by the fire. Tired, Esther carried her heavy pack up the narrow flight of stairs to her room in the round turret on the west side of the old house.

"Crepes!" She had left her window slightly open. Her curtain was soaked, and a puddle had gathered on her desk near her laptop and was dripping onto the floor. After closing the small wooden window, she ran for towels in the bathroom.

Once her floor was dry, she realized she hadn't seen her cat all night. "Miss Molly. Here kitty, kitty." She heard a soft meow coming from under her bed. She got down on the area rug and found Miss Molly hiding under the bed.

"You didn't like the lightning either, did you?" As if she had called for more. Lightning flashed, and thunder shook her third-floor room. Miss Molly screeched and flew into Esther's arms. Esther sat on the floor and stroked her until she purred softly. "Tonight is the night. I have put it off long enough. Tonight, I answer my bio-dad's letter. He wants me to forgive him, Miss Molly."

I've been praying. Trying. Why do I still have this feeling in the pit of my stomach when I think about it? Should I wait?

Esther kept a calendar on her phone. She opened it. At 8 p.m. she had scheduled homework. *Write back to Dad.* There it was in black and white.

"A promise to myself is a promise, Miss Molly. This is how we're going to beat Sophie for valedictorian. And it's how we are going to become someone and someday go someplace magical—doing the hard things. Maybe I'll write novels in Ireland? What do you think?"

Miss Molly didn't move. Her purring was so comforting Esther hated putting her down. Gently, she placed the cat on the area rug and went to her desk. Miss Molly had been alone too long. She followed and leapt onto the bed, then the nightstand, and easily to the desk where she perched and watched Esther.

Esther's phone vibrated in her pocket. She pulled it out.

> Text from Parker: *Hey beautiful. I had fun today.*
> Text to Parker: *Me too. Thanks so much for the tacos.*
> Text to Esther: *Anything for you. Headed to bed early so I can run in the morning. Night.*
> Text to Parker: *Night, night.*

She put the phone on the charger.
It vibrated again.

> Text from Sophie: *What the holy cheese wiz today, huh? Good luck tonight. I know it's the letter night.*
> Text to Sophie: *Thanks. I feel so bad for Nevaeh. If I were her, I'd be worried about small town gossip. Let's find her tomorrow and see if she's okay. Let's tell her we aren't going to gossip or post anything on social media. Night.*
> Text to Esther: *Agreed. We've seen how small-town gossip can turn into a social media frenzy. Night.*

Esther opened her organized desk drawer. On top of her journal was the now well-worn envelope. The return address was Point of Mountain Prison. She pulled out the single sheet of paper with neat handwriting. She had read and re-read it so many times, the creases in the folded paper were close to tearing.

Esther,

I have finally, really, found God. I am writing to tell you that I am sorry. I am sorry for not being there for you. I wish I could do all the things a father should do. I wish I had taught you to ride a bike or to drive. I can never change what I did. I have nothing to offer. All I can do is beg. I know I don't deserve it, but I am writing to ask for your forgiveness.

Love, Dad

Dad. He hadn't earned that title. Papa J had already been a better father than he ever had. Just reading the letter took Esther back to their last night together. She was hiding behind the red couch. He would soon be arrested for trying to kill her mother.

A single tear fell on the sheet of paper in her hand.

A promise is a promise. She set it down and pulled out a fresh, plain piece of printer paper.

Dear . . . "what do I call him?"

Dear Dad,

I am trying.

Esther

Then again, the sobs. Miss Molly climbed in her lap. Esther wrapped herself around Miss Molly. Lightning flashed. Thunder rumbled loud and long, rattling the windowpanes. The lights went out.

Nevaeh wasn't at school in the morning. Esther texted their informant, Bridget, who worked in the school office during first period. She said Angelica Rose had called Nevaeh in sick.

The day felt long to Esther. Especially when Mr. Kelly came to the library for the third time and they had to listen to his bad jokes and Ms. Priest's polite laughter.

"He must surf the net and memorize dad jokes for her," Sophie said. Esther snickered.

"Hurry, let's lock up. I want to get home and get ahead in all my classes." Esther dug out the library drawer key, locked the drawer, and turned off the first light.

"Nice try, E. I am already ahead and ready to focus on my next project." Sophie put her backpack on and turned off the rest of the lights as they headed for the door. The storm had blown over, and typical to the coast, it was twenty degrees warmer. It felt like a summer day.

"What project?"

"Project Dance Date," Sophie said.

"Who do you have in mind?"

"Elon Musk."

Esther laughed. "It's doable, but we will have to work fast. Aim high, right?" They were still chuckling when they left the library.

Esther was surprised to see her mom waiting for her. She had taken the soft top off the Jeep and was smiling at her over the back of the seat. Grace got out and handed Esther the car keys.

"I thought today would be perfect for driving lessons on the beach. All you have to do is drive five or so miles to the public beach access in Cabbott's Cove. Do you have your permit with you?"

Esther's mouth fell open and her heart began pounding in her chest. "That means we have to get on the highway."

"It isn't tourist season. The highway is two vacant lanes, except for log trucks and locals. Come on. No time like the present." Her mom didn't budge.

Esther looked at the keys. "I have to go to the bathroom."

Grace laughed her deep, throaty laugh. "That's nerves. There's one at the beach."

"I think I'll walk." Sophie stepped back.

"No way. You're next, Sophie. I texted your mom. I have permission to give you your first driving lesson."

Sophie's eyes were as round as her glasses. "Yes!" Her face split into a massive smile. She tossed her pack into the back of the Jeep. Climbing onto the large back wheel, she held onto the roll bar and plopped into the back seat. "Let's roll!"

Esther shook her head. "I think I'm going to puke."

"You got this! Shotgun. I always wanted to say that." Her mom snickered and got into the passenger's seat. "Come on, E. The parking lot is practically empty.

Ms. Priest waved and drove away. They were the last car left in the lot. Esther couldn't think of another excuse. She got in the driver's seat. Her mother talked her through how to use the clutch.

Finally, after five minutes of instructions and three minutes of mirror adjustments, it was time. Esther put her right foot on the brake, her left foot pushed in the clutch, and she examined the diagram on the shifter knob. She shifted into first.

"Now," her mom said. "Slowly, lift your foot off the clutch, and press the gas at the same time."

"At the same time?" Esther's mouth fell open, her eyebrows lifted, and she blinked rapidly, looking at her mother like she was crazy. "You know I'm not coordinated."

"You got this, E. You must have watched me drive before?" Her mother folded her arms and sat back.

Esther checked to make sure her hands were at ten and two. She gradually let the clutch out while putting her foot on the gas, and the car bucked. Not one, but two, three, four times, and then died.

To Esther's horror, her mother just laughed louder. "Everyone does that the first time."

After four more attempts, the Jeep slowly began to inch forward.

Esther remembered she also needed to steer the thing. She turned the wheel. For several minutes they just circled the parking lot in first gear and her mother explained, to Esther's horror, that as the Jeep went faster, she would need to shift into a higher gear.

"How do I do it?" Esther said.

She turned the wheel towards the exit and then stomped on the brake at the stop sign, killing the engine again. By this time, her mother was laughing so hard she had tears in the corners of her eyes.

She composed herself and said, "Okay. When you put your foot on the brake, you have to push in the clutch too."

Esther's palms were sweating. She looked in the rearview mirror and realized that Sophie's eyes were huge, and she had both arms wrapped around the roll bar on her mother's side of the car.

A log truck barreled past them, blowing her hair in her eyes.

"Okay, signal," her mother said. "You should signal three seconds before each intersection."

"While I work the clutch, the brake, the gas, and the steering wheel? At the same time?" Esther was breathing rapidly. She signaled.

"Take a deep breath and gently ease onto the highway."

Esther dumped the clutch and had to restart the car. Eventually, they rolled down the highway, hugging the shoulder. She drove ten miles below the speed limit and nothing her mother said could get her to drive any faster.

After what felt like an eternity, but was only ten minutes, they turned toward the beach.

"I'm getting it!" Esther shouted over the motor noise. "I signaled."

"Well done," her mother said. Her mother, however, held onto the bar on the dash with white knuckle hands.

"You didn't need to yell at me during that left turn, Mom."

"When I say stop, your foot had better hit that brake hard."

"Okay, but you really need to relax." Esther smiled. "I can do this."

"Pull over here. I need to lock the hubs in so we can use four-wheel drive on the beach."

Esther eased off the gravel road onto the sandy shoulder. When she turned the car off, her mother let out a loud breath. "Phew."

"My dad's car is all-wheel drive. He doesn't have to lock the hubs. Mom's goes into four-wheel drive with the push of a button," Sophie said.

"And your dad is a world-renowned scientist who can have any car he wants. Be smarter than me. Be a scientist." Grace locked in the last hub. She wiped the dirt from her hands on her jeans. "Your turn, Sophie."

"I've been watching. I'm ready." Confidently, Sophie accepted the keys. She and Esther traded places. When everyone was ready, Sophie cleared her throat, adjusted her glasses, and expertly drove them down the beach, on the sand, and later home without a hiccup.

When they pulled in front of Esther's house, windblown and laughing, Esther said, "Finally. Something you are definitely better at than me."

"Right? Well, wait until I get a prom date. Then I will be better at two things." Sophie winked at her and they giggled.

"Parker's coming over to work on the van tonight. Will we see you later?" Esther asked Sophie.

"What's for dinner?"

"Bake-it-yourself pizza," Grace said.

"Count me in. I'll be back after I walk the dog and practice my violin."

Grace and Esther gathered their things and put them on the lawn. Then Esther helped Grace snap the soft-top back on the Jeep.

"Mom? Would you mail something for me?" Esther asked. "Don't make a big deal of it, but I need a stamp for this." She pulled the letter to her father out of her backpack.

Her mother studied the address. "You don't need to tell me your reply. But can I ask you a question?"

"I guess."

"How do you feel about it?"

"I don't know. He asked me to forgive him. All I could say was, I'll try."

"I understand. He asked me to forgive him too after he tried to take you."

"I know. Why did you forgive him?"

Grace continued holding the envelope and running her fingers over the address for a minute. Then she looked at Esther and studied her face. She looked down and said, "To save myself. All the angry feelings and fear I had over what he had done were poisoning me. He isn't my problem now. He belongs to God, and I can't carry it anymore. I don't have to . . . I can't."

Esther felt the knot in her stomach twist as she thought about her mother's words. "I don't understand," Esther said.

"We should have talked about this sooner." Her mother looked at her with sad eyes. She gave Esther a half smile. "You're wiser than you think you are. One thing is for sure. You'll figure it out quicker than I did. Give me some time to think about your question."

Chapter Four

Who's on Your Dance Card?

After the last pizza plates were cleared, Esther, Sophie, and Nephi went with Papa J to the garage. The garage was next door to Nephi and Grandma Mable's apartment, on the back of the house. It went from the kitchen into their bedrooms and down in the lower level of their old Victorian home.

Bridget, Parker, and Paisley showed up a few minutes after the garage door was up and the lights were on. They had been working for a few months on Parker's 1964 seventeen-window VW van. It was a gift from a family friend that they were turning into a surf mobile.

Papa J gave them a quick lesson, and they watched a YouTube tutorial on sanding down Bondo, which was used to fill the little dents and dings. Using crates, rolling carts, and chairs, they sat around the van sanding and chatting. It had become their place. A place to go and just be together.

Paisley had the vinyl for the seats on the floor nearby. Bridget was helping her cut out pieces using a pattern she'd made from the old upholstery.

"You should have seen Sophie drive. She's a natural." Esther dipped her sandpaper block in a bucket of water and made random patterns on the body of the van next to Parker.

"It's all those years of video games. I had one with a steering wheel," Sophie said.

Esther laughed. "If that was the case, Nephi would be a NASCAR champion."

"Who needs to go to NASCAR when we have this sweet ride." While concentrating on sanding, Nephi stuck his tongue out, making Esther laugh.

"Right?" Parker reached over and gave Nephi a buddy push.

"What are you guys doing this weekend?" Nephi asked.

"Sleeping in." Paisley looked up from her project and smiled.

Out of the blue and completely changing the subject, Parker asked, "Esther, can we do a late dinner after the dance at my house? Nephi and I have a plan."

Before Esther could respond, Sophie said, "Hey! Did you even ask her if she wants to go with you?"

Esther's mouth fell open, and her eyes grew as she looked back and forth between Parker and Sophie. Parker was scowling, and Sophie had dropped her sandpaper and had her hands on her hips.

Esther held up her free hand and said, "Whoa. It's okay, Sophie. Who else would I go with?"

"Humph." Sophie stuck her nose up in the air but didn't back down. "Don't neglect your date, Parker. You too, Nephi. You're lucky to have someone who will go with you." She turned her back on them and left the garage.

Esther dropped her sandpaper and followed her out the door. "Sophie! Don't go."

"Sorry," Sophie said. Her arms were folded, and she frowned.

"You don't look sorry."

"I'm not!" She held her hands out, like she was pleading her case. "Don't let him take you for granted."

"He doesn't."

"*Today's Teen Magazine* says a good date brings you flowers and asks you out in creative ways."

"I told you not to read that stuff. You're too smart for it."

Deflated, Sophie said, "It's all I have. Dating Ransom was like watching Ransom admire himself and trying not to ruin his selfies and videos. He was so into himself it wasn't a positive experience. The entire time we were together, all he did was text and laugh at things girls sent him. The only other people I've watched date are your parents, you, and Nephi."

Esther realized Parker was at the door to the garage.

Frowning, he was wiping his hands on a rag. Without looking up, he asked, "Is everything okay?"

She ignored him and turned back to Sophie. "Thanks for having my back, girl. But we have got to work on your coaching skills."

Sophie chuckled softly. Arm in arm, they walked back toward the garage.

"Did I do something wrong?" Parker studied her face.

"Men." Sophie shook her head and went back in the garage.

Papa J watched silently.

Esther turned her back on Papa J for some privacy and tried to smile. "She's still upset about Ransom. He didn't treat her very well. And honestly, she thinks you should have asked me to the dance." She shrugged. "But it's okay. Who else would I go with?"

"She's right," Parker said. "But honestly, just tell me next time, okay? You don't have to be afraid to talk to me."

His words hit her in the gut. She looked down at the ground. "You know it's hard for me to trust."

"What can I do to help?" Parker asked.

"Nothing. It's my fault," Esther said. She looked over her shoulder and saw Papa J, still watching. "We can talk later."

"Okay," Parker said. "But please, can we talk about how we can build trust between us?"

"Papa J is watching."

"What can I do to make up for not asking you and assuming you'd go?" Parker asked.

"Would anyone like some ice cream? I can bring it down?" Esther said loudly. She forced a smile and walked up the gravel path to the house without replying to his question.

Later, while they took an ice-cream break, Sophie scrolled through her social media. Nephi and Paisley were teasing each other. Bridget was explaining to Esther and Parker how a combustion motor worked.

Papa J had his head down. He was sanding the side door of the van, working away.

"Whoa! Guys. Guys. Look at this." Sophie held her phone up. They gathered together and passed it around the group.

It was a post by Baxter Jones.

You think you are so much better than we are. You don't know anything. Thanks for ruining our lives. You arrogant rich kids have a stench that makes me want to puke. You have everything and you hate anyone who isn't like YOU. I hope this Halloween is more tricks and the only treat you get is from me! I hope you burn like you burned us!

There was a picture of Oceanside High on fire. It was hand drawn, like the picture of Paisley. The thing that alarmed Esther most was seeing Paisley and Nephi's faces or faces that were similar, in the tiny, penciled library windows.

"Give me that." Papa J took the phone. He read it for a minute. Frowning, he used his own phone to make a call and walked out of the garage. Esther heard him say, "Hello, Chief?"

Parker cleaned up and quietly left for home with Paisley, while Papa J was still on the phone.

Nephi kept working, calm and collected as usual. Esther and Sophie watched Papa J pace in front of the garage. Esther's mouth hung open as she tried to hear what he was saying. She only caught every other word, but his tone was unmistakably fierce.

"Can you imagine him chasing you down and arresting you? Does he lift weights? What do you feed him?" Sophie flexed one of her tiny arms and checked out her own muscles. On her four-foot-eleven-inch frame, it looked ridiculous. Esther snickered. Papa J spun around and gave them a stern look with his finger on his lips. Clearly, they weren't to interrupt.

"Holy cheese wiz. I've never seen him like this. What is he? Six foot three?" Sophie asked.

"Four. Six foot four, two hundred pounds of lean American muscle in the shape of a brick with legs. I hope he never gets this mad at me," Esther said.

Finally, he ended the call and put Sophie's phone in his pocket. But he didn't stop pacing. He took out Sophie's phone and tried to unlock it. Then he rubbed his hair again and seemed lost in thought.

Sophie held out her hand. "Papa J? My phone?"

"Oh, sorry." He handed her the phone and took his cell out of his front pocket. He called someone else. With the phone to his ear, he went back to pacing.

"It's late. Do you want me to walk you home?" Esther looked at Sophie.

"I wouldn't miss this for the world."

Nephi joined them at the garage door. "Is he still on the phone?"

"Yup." Esther realized they must look odd. All three of their heads followed Papa J, back and forth, back and forth. "Should we finish cleaning up?" They went back into the garage and Esther started sweeping around the van and dumping buckets of gray water into the dirty shop sink. But every once in a while, she'd look up. *Still pacing.*

Everything was wrapped up, and they all met at the light switch.

"Okay. We need to talk to your mom." Just like that, Papa J was back. "Lock the lights and turn off the door. I mean—lock the door and turn off the lights." He took the gravel path around the house to the front door.

They locked up and quietly followed him. The path wrapped around the large Victorian and the second detached garage, a free-standing building that was like a storage shed. It held everything that they thought they might need, but never seemed to be able to find. Just past the wooden garage, the path ran in front of the large front porch. Papa J easily took the twelve steps to the porch two and three at a time.

Sophie grabbed Esther's arm and made a face with her brows up and mouth open. "Have you ever seen him like this? Scary dad?"

"Scary as in bad dad? No. He looks worried," Esther said.

Papa J was back on the phone when they got to the living room. Esther's mother was reading by the fire and Mable was watching a show. She turned the television off and stared at Papa J's serious face.

He ended the call and squatted in front of her mom's chair so they were facing each other. His intense blue eyes narrowed and his mouth was in a firm line. "Okay, Grace, I don't want you to worry, but I'm concerned."

Esther's mother's book came down and her eyebrows raised. She tilted her head. "What happened, Hart? Nephi? What did you do?" She turned on Nephi, her brother.

Raising both hands, Nephi said, "I didn't do anything?"

Grandma Mable said, "Nephi?"

"No. It isn't Nephi." Papa J stood up. He pulled the other winged-back chair by the fireplace closer to Esther's mom. "Look at this." He pulled his phone out and opened it. "Wait. Sophie, text the screen-shots I took of the post to me." He gave Sophie his number. Then he showed Grace the photos.

"Wow. What happened to this kid? Nephi, do you know him? That looks like your face. But who are the rich kids he's talking about?" Grace zoomed in on the picture. "Paisley?"

"We aren't rich." Nephi gave Esther a crooked smile.

"Yes, but someone looking at the size of this house might think so. Or someone who has a lot less than you do. It's all relative." Grace handed Papa J back his phone.

"I called the chief and sent him screenshots from Sophie's phone. We're going to the school in the morning and assessing the threat."

Esther heard a sharp intake of breath and realized it was Sophie. She had folded her small arms and was shaking her head. "Jackson and Bubba, I mean Baxter, do everything together, If they get into trouble for this online post after the fight at school with Nephi and Paisley, it will be like throwing Sriracha sauce on baby food."

"Sophie's right," Esther said. Concern sat like a rock in her stomach. "You don't know them. They can be really mean."

Papa J leaned forward, his elbows on his knees, and looked at Esther with sincere eyes. "That's just the point. I don't know them, and we don't know what they're capable of. We're going to find out. School threats have to be taken seriously."

"I can take care of them." Nephi grinned and stuck his chest out.

Grandma Mable got up and softly smacked Nephi's backside with the back of her hand. "That's what started this. Haven't you spent enough time in Principal Kelly's office? Do I have to get another call from the office and hear you're in trouble again? You're over eighteen now. You could make a permanent record for yourself. Sit down and give Hart your respect."

Nephi looked like a whipped puppy. He plopped onto one end of the couch and folded his arms, scowling.

Esther's phone rang. It was Parker. She sent it to voicemail.

"It's like he's threatening to but hasn't directly said it. Legally, does this fall under free speech?" Grace was looking intently at the phone. "Is there anything law enforcement can do?"

"Are you kidding? Did you see the picture?" It was a redundant question. Sophie jumped up, but she was so short it didn't have the impact she wanted.

Papa J's head dropped. He was frowning when he looked back up. "Chief said the same thing. It's borderline. Honestly, it depends on what he says during the interview."

Parker called Esther again. Once more, she sent him to voicemail.

"I put a call into Principal Kelly. We'll know more tomorrow. The reason I wanted to talk to you is I don't want any of you in school until we sort this out. I'm calling Parker's parents and Bridget's mom too."

Esther leaped to her feet. "But I have class. I have gym. I don't want to fail a no-brainer like gym! And I need to see Parker."

"Esther." That was all her mother had to say. She didn't even need to raise her voice. It was the glaring look on her face that spoke volumes. Esther slowly sat down.

"Hart," her mom said, "we're going to follow your advice."

Esther stood again. Esther's mother glared at her. Esther sat slowly back down.

"Don't worry. I'll bring home your homework," Sophie said.

"I also texted your parents, Sophie, and we spoke for a moment. They agree with me. They asked if Grandma Mable could take care of you tomorrow," Papa J said.

"Crepes! I'm not a baby. I don't need a sitter."

"Well, then, don't act like one." Mable raised one eyebrow at Sophie and then winked. "Don't worry. We'll have fun. We'll work on Esther's driving."

Esther held up her hands. "No! I can call a cab. I don't need to drive."

Her mother stood up. "All right, my big happy family. This advocate needs her beauty sleep before the phone starts ringing. Everyone to bed. Nephi, walk Sophie down the block to her house?"

"Do I have . . ." One look from Mable and Esther watched the coin drop. Nephi shook his head and got up. "Come on, Sophie."

Esther tried to call Parker. It went straight to voicemail. She texted him, *Call me again.*

Sleep eluded Esther. She just watched her cell phone, while Miss Molly slept on her hair. No matter where she moved, somehow Molly would manage to snuggle in and purr like a motor. The sun was rising, and the birds were singing when she finally gave up and sat up, waking Molly. She wanted to throw the phone across the room.

6 a.m. Too early to text. Please text. Please text. Just call back and tell me we're okay. My heart actually hurts. I didn't know I could feel this way. Is this what love feels like? Did Mom hurt like this with Dad? It's like having a piece of yourself carved out with a melon baller. I hate this.

"I'm too young for this, Molly. This wasn't on my schedule until my junior year of college—in a town far, far away." The cat gave her a wary look and burrowed under the covers, disappearing completely. "Fine. You're ignoring me too? I don't blame you."

Her phone vibrated in her hand. It was a text from Parker, and it felt like electric paddles jumpstarting her heart. She held her breath while she read it.

Hey. Sorry I didn't text or call again last night. You didn't answer. Fell asleep. Why didn't you answer?

She always answered. In seconds she would answer every call, every text. *Does he think I put him off on purpose?*

She hastily replied.

I tried. No voicemail. Papa J and Mom were talking to us. They are making us stay home today because of a post Bubba made. They were talking and I couldn't call back. It was kind of intense. I'm so sorry. Can you call me now?

She craved his voice, to know they were okay, and that he would still look at her with light in his eyes and laugh with her about the silly little things they shared.

Text from Parker: *Wish. Was worried. Feel bad. I am sorry. Please forgive me.*

"Esther," Mary whispered through the keyhole in Esther's door. She knocked softly. "Essy. Let me in."

"Not now." Annoyed, Esther reread his text. There were those words again, forgive me. *For what? I'm the one who didn't answer the phone. I should say I'm sorry.*

Text to Parker: *For what? It's my fault. Talk later?*

Little fists knocked harder. "Esther . . . I want to snuggle. Essy. Open up, Essy."

"Just a minute, Mary." She couldn't think. Mary knocked, and he didn't reply. A full minute passed. *Maybe he lost service? Why doesn't he reply?*

Text to Parker: *Are you there?*

"Let me in." Her little fists kept tapping non-stop.

Text to Esther: *Oh. I thought talk later meant you had to go.*

What should I say? Something is wrong. I guess I'm kind of upset he didn't ask me to the dance. Her pulse sounded like rushing water in her ears. A little voice, still, small, whispered to her heart. *Risk.*

"Esther!" She got up and, without looking up from her phone, opened the door. She stayed standing by the door. Mary passed her on a dead run and jumped on her bed, burrowing under the covers. Miss Molly burrowed out and ran for the door, her claws skittering around the corner and down the hall.

Text to Parker: *I just wanted to hear your voice. I hoped we could talk.*

Text to Esther: *Me too. Already stuck in the car with Mom, Meredith, Bridget, and Paisley. Going to Portland to power shop for the dance this weekend. Ugh. Dad didn't want me home alone because of the stupid stuff online.*

"Molly left," Mary said. Esther, still standing by the door, glanced up and saw Mary sitting in the covers and pouting

Text to Parker: *Sorry about Papa J*

Text to Esther: *I don't want you at school. Protective. E? Will you still go to the dance with me? Not the way I should have asked.*

She felt all the pressure release. *Of course he cares about me. I'm such a goof. Why do I get like this? I need to trust more.*

Text to Parker: *I would be so happy to go with you.*

"Make her come back, Essy." Mary started jumping on her bed.

Text to Esther: *Hitting mountain. No service for a while. TTYL*

Then a new thought struck Esther squarely between her eyes, "What will I wear to the dance, Mary?"

Esther ran across the room and jumped on the bed with Mary, who started giggling hysterically.

"Girls!" Esther's mom called from inside her bedroom.

Esther laughed, closed her door, and jumped back into her warm bed with Mary.

"Tell me a story." Mary rolled into a ball and looked at her with her pale blue eyes. She twisted a dark blonde curl around her finger.

Esther thought for a moment. A smile born from a good idea lit up her face. "Okay . . ."

Esther sat up. The story formulated in her mind in a minute. She saw it play out in fast motion and then it was real. "Hark and listen to the tale of Oceanside's haunted library and the librarian who was checked out of life. Once upon a time, there was a librarian who liked to encourage children to come into her library and read. Once in her lair, she would sit by the fire and read the children stories while feeding them cookies and candy, fattening them up for All Hallows Eve. She would pile them up with stacks of books. More than any little girl or boy should check out."

Mary sat up, smiling. "I like her."

"She had black hair and black eyes. She wore a white apron. She had words written all over her crisp white apron. The kind of words that fell out of books and kept you up at night. Words like *vampire, zombie, prince,* and *true love.* She carried a date stamp and when you checked your books out, she would stamp a card and say, 'Return your books on time or be checked out forever . . .' So, when the day was done and the last book was checked out, the library caught fire."

"Oh, no." Mary's eyes grew wide. Esther made the sounds of fire. Mary was entranced.

"When the firemen came to put it out, they didn't find any sign of the librarian. Some say she was reshelved to the great library in heaven. But others say, that when the Oceanside High Library is dark and quiet, you can hear her say, 'Past due . . . Past due . . . I'm coming for you!" Esther jumped and tickled Mary who dissolved into laughter and then ran screaming from her room to her mother's room.

A few hours later, Esther, Nephi, and Sophie sat around the kitchen table helping Esther's mom put together dance tickets. Esther's mother had signed up for the job with the boosters, and somehow it was now the family's job.

"I think we should go to the thrift store after this and find costumes for the ball. I finished my entire week's homework assignments."

"A thrift store is a great place to look for costumes. We should dig in the attic too," Esther said.

Sophie examined her attempt at crafting a dance ticket per Paisley's instructions. She'd cut out paper in the shape of a mask with the ticket printed on it and taped a popsicle stick to one side. If you held it up, it was like an old-fashioned mask. Cutting out the eye holes was taking them forever.

"Do we have to cut out the eyes?" Esther asked.

"It's Paisley's design. I think they're adorable. Only twenty more to go." Her mother was stacking the finished masks in a box after numbering them. "Paisley is really creative. You should hear what she and the boosters have planned for the Halloween Haunted House and fundraiser."

"Are you and Papa J going to help with the haunted house?" Esther asked her mother.

"I've volunteered to bake for the bake sale."

The front door to the house opened and Esther got up to see who had come in. Papa J hung up his police coat and gear in the closet by the door.

"How did it go with Baxter?" Esther asked.

He shook his head. "Where's your mom?"

"In here," her mom called from the kitchen.

"How does she do that?" Esther smiled.

"Superhuman mom hearing." Papa J winked back at her.

They went to the kitchen, and she went back to work. Papa J dug in the fridge and came out with a Diet Coke. He cracked it open. "Jackson and Baxter are both over eighteen, so I can tell you because he isn't a juvenile. I guess Jackson had no idea Baxter had posted the drawing he made. He admitted to making it the day he was angry, but he said he wasn't mad anymore and would never do anything like that. I still wonder . . ." He took a sip of his drink.

"What do you think, really?" Esther's mom asked.

He shrugged. "The jury is still out on Jackson. Jackson did draw the picture and give it to Baxter. But the pencil drawing isn't a crime. Baxter posted it and insisted Jackson didn't know. But Baxter is Jackson's best friend, so of course he would protect Jackson. Because Baxter posted a threatening picture, Principal Kelly suspended him for two days. Legally, because he didn't make any specific threats and he backed right down when we were talking, there wasn't a crime and we, the police, couldn't do anything. He said he was just blowing off steam. I tend to think he's a really angry kid, and Jackson is the only friend he has. I think Jackson was involved. I feel really sorry for Baxter. Jackson's life is pretty awful too."

"Why? What's wrong with their lives?" Esther wanted to know. Papa J had seen a lot as a police officer, so if he thought something was awful, then it must be worse than the normal person could imagine.

He shrugged and gave her a sad smile. "It's his story and not mine to tell. You don't need to worry. You can go back to school when you decorate for the ball. That will give it all time to die down."

"Maybe it's his own fault that life is awful. I mean, seriously. No one wants to hang out with someone who is always cranky and smells like three-day-old dirty diapers," Sophie said.

"Don't judge a diaper until you check the contents," Esther's mom said.

There was a knock on the front door.

Mary, who was wearing red and white striped onesie pajamas, bolted for the door. The vinyl feet in her pajamas caused her to lose control on the wood floor and slam into the door. Knowing Mary shouldn't open the door to strangers, Esther ran after her.

Mary hung on the doorknob until it turned and opened, just as Esther arrived. "Ironpot!" Mary opened the screen and hugged the large police officer around his ample middle.

"Hi. Are you here to see Papa J?" Esther held the door open. Ironpot took off his police baseball cap and came in with his hat in his hands. He wasn't his usual smiley self. His brows were drawn together, and he only gave her a weak half-smile.

"Is he here?"

"Papa J!" Mary yelled, running back toward the kitchen, not having learned her lesson about slipping on the slick floors. When she tried to turn at the fireplace, she passed behind it and they heard a crash—glass.

"I'm here." Papa J came into the living room. "Esther, can you help your mom sweep up the glass before someone gets cut?"

"Sure." Esther hung back, worried about the ominous feeling rolling off Ironpot.

"I wanted to fill you in on what I know about Jackson Green and Baxter Jones," Ironpot said to Papa J. "Can we step outside?"

"Can I listen?" Esther asked.

Ironpot didn't respond. He just looked down. Papa J put a hand on her shoulder. "Not this time. I know you and Sophie love to investigate, and have inquisitive minds, but this time I need to speak to Ironpot alone."

Ironpot's shoulders seemed to relax, and he let out a long breath. He looked at Esther and smiled weakly, put his hat on, and the two men stepped out onto the porch.

This is killing me. I have to know. After all, it's making life a mess for all of us. Esther put her ear to the window on the door to see if she could hear anything. She couldn't see them through the glass, so maybe they had left the porch. All she heard were muffled voices.

"E! I could use some help," Grandma Mable poked her head into the living room. Esther sighed and went to sweep up the glass.

Chapter Five

The Refreshment Committee

Later that night, Nephi drove Esther and Sophie to the Sweet Treat Shop in Cabbott's Cove where they planned to meet Parker, Paisley, and Bridget at Nevaeh's mother's quaint store. The tall building sat on Main Street between two other historic buildings and had gray shingle siding. But the trim, doors, windows, and window boxes were all painted to look like candy.

Esther knocked, and they waited outside the peppermint pink back door.

Sophie studied the candy-covered building. "Don't you feel like we are Hansel and Gretel going into the witch's house in the woods and she's going to fatten us up to eat us?"

"Not you," Nephi said. "You would just be an after-dinner mint. Hardly worth the three tons of food it would take to maintain your current weight of sixty pounds."

"Very funny. You, on the other hand, would be over two hundred pounds of prime chocolate fudge." Sophie gave Nephi a friendly push.

Laughing, Esther waved at Parker, Paisley, and Bridget, who were crossing the parking lot to join them.

Another car pulled into the back parking lot. It was a maroon family van with a sticker on the back. The sticker was a picture of stick figures of a mom, a dad, and more than twenty kids for the foster kids the Ironpots had parented, and a dog, a cat, and a chicken.

Jackson Green and Bubba Jones unfolded their tall bodies and got out the van's side door.

"I don't get why they're allowed to help?" Sophie said.

"Helping with the dance is their consequence. I guess this is a part of the project," Esther said.

The driver's side window opened, and Mrs. Ironpot leaned out. "I'll be back in two hours, unless you call me. Don't forget to wash your hands and say thank you!" She turned the van around and left them standing awkwardly facing Esther and her friends.

"Let's get this over with," Jackson said as he brushed past Esther and tried the door. It was still locked. He banged on it twice, loudly.

Nevaeh came out with a huge smile on her happy face. "Welcome to the home of sweet treats and mountains of candy." She held the door, letting everyone shuffle into the warm kitchen. Her mother, Angelica, was dressed in a pink jogging suit covered by an apron that looked like a large birthday cake with candles for straps.

"Welcome! We're ready for you. There is a lot to do. Nevaeh will get you aprons, gloves, and hairnets. Meet her at the handwashing sink." She pointed to a back corner where Nevaeh stood next to a sink with aprons over one arm and the water already running.

They lined up and washed their hands. Esther felt Parker's touch on her shoulders. She leaned back into his chest for just a second and then turned and smiled. He returned a smile so warm her stomach fluttered, her heart beat a little harder, and she felt joy color her cheeks red.

She and Parker didn't get a chance to talk. She and Sophie were working with Nevaeh on the deadly taffy machine while he was helping Paisley make candy.

Esther's eyes kept wandering to Parker. He was laughing with Paisley, his twin, while they made chocolate turtles under the direction of Fred, a shop employee. He was a short, round man who looked like he belonged in a chocolate factory singing with Oompa Loompas. He wore all white, including a chef's hat. After a few minutes with Paisley, his white apron was covered in brown spots.

"Good grief, Ms. Stuart. It isn't difficult," Fred said in frustration.

"Speak for yourself." Paisley threw her spatula back in the chocolate, sending a spray of brown across Fred's round red face.

"Paisley!" Parker said. He shrugged and chuckled.

"I hardly find that entertaining," Fred said, and went back to explaining how to make turtles with caramel and chocolate.

"Esther! Lookout." Nevaeh pushed her hand. She stumbled back and bumped into Sophie. "You almost got your apron string caught in the machine. You can't look away."

Esther and Sophie gave Nevaeh their full attention. Nevaeh's eyes were as big as saucers. "All right. One more time. This is the taffy puller and wrapper."

The red and white machine looked old. It was made of heavily painted steel. The electronic motor made a shook-shook sound that was so loud Nevaeh had to shout to be heard. The machine rapidly pulled, sliced, wrapped, and spit taffy.

Nevaeh held up her hand for their full attention. "The puller can grab your strings and pull you in and choke you, or worse. It could flay the flesh right off your arm. You must focus. I'll load the candy in this end, and you'll sort the pieces into the gift bags on the other end. We want at least two of each kind in each bag. I have boxes containing three hundred empty bags or two to three bags for each student and chaperone."

Bridget was stirring a witch's cauldron. Not far from Parker and Paisley was at a bank of six burners, all low to the floor and large. Each had a stainless-steel pot warming with chocolate and other sweets. Bridget held a large wooden paddle and stirred.

"Where are Jackson and Bubba?" Sophie asked Nevaeh.

"Over there." Nevaeh motioned behind her and in the corner. Through a slightly open door, they could see a small room with a table. The table had a large marble slab on top. It held ten or twelve trays of caramel apples. Every tray of apples was decorated differently. It looked like Angelica was giving them directions on how to roll the dipped apples in sprinkles and crushed cookies.

Jackson's arms were folded. Bubba had his hands on his hips. Almost as if he could feel the burn of Esther's eyes, Bubba raised his face and met her stare with his watery, gray eyes. He smirked, exposing his yellow teeth.

Nevaeh's hands shook as she wrestled with the candy. Esther noticed sweat on her forehead and that she was breathing hard.

"Can I help?" Esther asked, loud enough to be heard.

Nevaeh smiled, and it made the dark circles under her eyes crinkle. "Nope! Just bag it!"

Esther and Sophie worked in silence with the machine pumping. Someone turned on KLAM, the classic rock station, and they listened to River Peace play the hits from the nineties.

By the time they were finished, Esther had learned how to bag taffy, make a few chocolates, and had worked with Sophie to make more than three hundred treat bags.

Esther shouted to Nevaeh, "Are we close to done?"

Nevaeh turned the taffy maker off. "Yup. Just have to clean up the machine."

Angelica joined the group, followed by Jackson and Bubba, who were both eating candied apples. Esther watched Angelica give both boys a full bag of taffy.

"Thanks, everyone," Angelica said. "You've been great. Now, Fred, Nevaeh, and I can finish cleaning up. Give your folks a call."

Sophie walked over to Jackson and looked up at his face. "Why did the Ironpots bring you?"

"None of your business, shorty." Jackson frowned and turned his back on her.

"They are our friends, too," Bubba said to Sophie.

I'm going to ask Papa J. Maybe they were foster kids? I wonder if the Ironpots took care of Bubba and Jackson at one time? I know they don't live with them now.

"Sophie. Let it go." Esther looked at Sophie and they exchanged a look of understanding. Esther took out her phone and texted Papa J. He worked with Ironpot. He would know.

> Text to Papa J: *Why did the Ironpots give Jackson and Bubba a ride down to the treat shop?*
> Text to Esther: *I told you. That's their story.*
> Text to Papa J: *Were they in foster care?*

No answer. Sophie was looking over her shoulder. "He's said that a lot lately. I wonder what that means exactly?"

"I guess it means whatever happened is confidential." She put her phone away. Nevaeh was at the door talking to Parker. "Sophie, let's go talk to Nevaeh while we have time."

Sophie nodded. They dropped their aprons in a laundry hamper near the sink. Nevaeh and Parker were laughing when they joined them.

"I was just asking Nevaeh how she kept from eating everything in sight." Parker grinned and Nevaeh blushed.

"You can actually get sick of candy. The only thing that tempts me is the caramel apples, and it isn't for the caramel." Nevaeh grinned from ear to ear.

"No! I don't believe you. I have eaten a whole pillowcase of Halloween candy and loved every bite." Sophie rubbed her tiny, flat stomach.

"You could eat an elephant and ask for seconds." Esther shook her head. "If I tried to keep up with you on pizza night, I would be barfing."

"Did someone say pizza? I'm starving. Let's go." Nephi shook car keys. Esther gave Parker a quick hug.

Esther whispered to Nephi, "I need to talk to Nevaeh first."

"Nevaeh?" Esther nudged Sophie and reached out to touch Nevaeh. "Do you have a minute? Can we talk outside?"

Nevaeh tilted her head and raised her eyebrows, questioning, but said, "Okay . . ." She stepped through the backdoor. Esther and Sophie followed her.

Nephi passed them and headed for his truck. "Don't take too long. I'm starving."

"Hey! That's my line," Sophie called after him.

Parker and Paisley came out. Parker gave Esther another quick hug and whispered in her ear, "Call you later?"

She nodded and turned her attention to Nevaeh, whose entire demeanor had changed. Her arms were folded across her chest, her mouth was drawn into a tight straight line. She stood tall, feet spread, defensive.

Esther wasn't sure where they should start. *She looks angry.*

"Listen, Nevaeh," Sophie jumped in. "We just wanted to let you know that we know what it's like to live in a small town and have people talk about you. We don't want you to worry about us passing on any gossip or saying anything about what happened at the meeting the other night."

Esther studied Nevaeh's face. "We promise. Life can be a train wreck sometimes. I've had my personal life gossiped about all over social media," Esther said.

As if she was unable to keep eye contact, Nevaeh looked down. "Sorry. I mean, thanks, I guess. The whole thing just surprised me."

"It surprised us all," Sophie chuckled. "I never thought about Ms. Priest . . ."

Esther leaned toward Sophie and gently bumped her to get her to stop talking.

"Yeah," Nevaeh said. She looked up as Jackson and Bubba passed them and climbed into Ironpot's van and left. Nephi was in his truck, talking on the phone with the engine running. Nevaeh closed the shop door, so they were alone under the back porch light in the dark parking lot. "It's just that I've lost a lot." It sounded like she was choking when she said the last few words.

"Where's your dad?" Sophie asked.

Nevaeh looked up from under hooded eyes. Even in the dim light, Esther could see her face was swimming with emotion. Her arms tightened their hold on her middle. She took a deep breath.

Looking at Esther, Nevaeh said, "I think you might get it. Angelica was my nanny when my mom died. I was nine. Dad was considering marrying Angelica and then the house caught fire. My dad died in the fire. Luckily, Angelica pulled me out of the house before I died and stayed with me.

"I was old enough they accused me of playing with matches and starting the fire. I don't know what I would have done without Angelica going to bat for me and being willing to become a foster parent. It was my dad's lawyer's idea to ask Angelica to care for me and my dad's money permanently."

"Kids make mistakes. What made them think you lit the fire?" Esther asked.

"It started in two places, and they found a box of wooden matches in my room. Angelica sometimes let me light a candle for my mom, with her supervision of course, so I had some matches in my nightstand."

"Did they find out who started it?" Sophie asked.

"No. They looked at people that worked for my dad, but they never arrested anyone."

"That's awful. Did Angelica think you lit the fire?" Esther asked.

"No. She never asked me anyway," Nevaeh said. "Angelica's been here for me, you know? She's my mom. She adopted me."

"Is that why she moved you here?" Esther said.

"No. We lived in California for a while. She remarried this really cool guy that owned a software company. But then he died when his private plane went down. Life has been really hard for her. I do my best to help out, but she gets sad."

"Oh, Nevaeh." Esther felt her own heart would burst, just listening. "That doesn't even compare to my experience. That is a lot of loss—too much."

"Sheesh. That's like Lifetime TV loss," Sophie said softly.

Nevaeh chuckled, but she didn't smile. She looked down at the ground and shook her head. "Anyway. I just really want Angelica to be happy, after all she's done for me. I wasn't an easy kid after my dad died. I was pretty messed up. She really liked Aiden . . .I guess I did too."

"Men." Sophie shook her head.

Esther gave Sophie a sharp glance. Sophie shrugged.

"Nevaeh!" The back door opened, and Angelica stood framed by the inside light. A blast of hot air and sweet smells flooded the parking lot.

"I guess I better help clean up." Nevaeh's arms fell to her side, and she gave the girls a sad smile.

"Can we help?" Esther asked softly, but Nevaeh just shook her head no.

"See you at the dance decorating party tomorrow," Sophie called to Nevaeh's retreating figure.

Esther leaned close to Sophie. "Part of me wonders if she did light the fire and part of me thinks she's great and there's no way. What do you think?"

"Famous last words by neighbors and friends of serial killers. 'He was a nice guy.' If this were a sappy movie, Angelica would have lit the fire and blamed the orphan."

"What if she blamed her and then used her status as a foster mom and wonderful person to avoid suspicion? But then, she didn't inherit," Esther said.

"No. But she does control Nevaeh's money. I wonder what happens if Nevaeh dies before eighteen?"

"And, is Angelica lying to Nevaeh. What if there is still a lot of money?"

Nephi leaned out the car window. "The only mystery here, is where's my pizza. You call it in and I'll buy when we get to town."

Chapter Six

The Decorating Committee

Esther and Sophie pushed open the doors to a very different library when they returned to school. The soundtrack to an instrumental version of *The Phantom of the Opera* musical was playing. Parker's parents were setting up a tall ladder under the fifteen-foot ceiling, in the middle of the bookshelves. A man in a gas company uniform was checking something inside the fireplace, and Madison Merriweather was standing over him. It sounded like she was giving him a constant string of advice.

Aiden Van Doren and River Peace had moved two of the massive shelves and opened a space for dancing by the east windows. The music was coming from a small speaker while River and Aiden were detangling what seemed to be miles of cords and wire. Two speaker towers waited.

"Whoa. They obviously haven't entered this century. You don't need a whole building for a computer or a small coffin for a speaker," Sophie said. She peeled her backpack off and threw it under the library counter.

Esther kept her hoodie on and looked for Parker in the chaos. "I don't see Parker."

"Didn't you two get to talk last night?" Sophie asked. "Has he officially asked you to the ball?"

"Yes, he asked me," Esther said and walked away before Sophie asked how. *I am not telling her it was by text or that we didn't talk, and he didn't call me. She'll go after him.*

"Wait just one minute." Sophie followed her to the fireplace. "Spill."

"We just talked. He apologized and asked me to go."

"When did this happen?"

"The night after the fight or whatever it was."

"Why didn't you tell me?" Sophie's eyes narrowed, and she studied Esther's face, skeptically.

"It wasn't important." *I am not telling, and I still don't know what we're doing for dinner.* Esther stepped closer to the author, Madison Merriweather. "Hi. Is there something we can do to help?"

"Oh, no, my darling. We are . . ." Madison gasped in delight as, at that very moment, the gas log the technician had just installed lit up and fire licked the natural-looking log replicas. "Beautiful!"

"That should do it." The technician stood up, signed some papers, and handed them to Madison. She signed and he gathered his tools.

"Oh! It's lovely," Ms. Priest said. She crossed the room. She was dressed more casually than Esther had ever seen before. She was in jeans and a black t-shirt and white tennis shoes.

Esther felt a cold breeze ruffle her hair. She looked up just in time to see Paisley and Parker open the doors with Jackson hot on Paisley's heels.

"I'm sorry," Jackson said. He frowned underneath his shaggy, dark hair.

Paisley stopped walking and faced Jackson, hands on her hips. She emphasized every word with an angry pointer finger. "I don't understand, Jackson. You know I'm dating Nephi. Why would you even ask?"

Bubba came in, just in time to hear Paisley tell Jackson. "You just need to leave me alone, Jackson Green. Once this dance is over, you will give me space. I have no interest in you. I'm dating Nephi."

"Paisley!" Mrs. Stuart was climbing down the ladder, her lips set tight.

Paisley looked at her mother, folded her arms, and headed toward her. She crossed the room with her nose in the air. It was the mean girl look Esther had learned was a cover for her underlying feelings.

Esther winced when she saw a look of pain cross Jackson's face. He folded his arms. His long plaid flannel sleeves were over his hands and torn. He actually wiped a tear from one eye and turned, running into Bubba.

"Let's go."

Bubba snarled at Paisley, "You . . ." He swore at Paisley, and Esther gasped. Paisley scowled at him. Her mother said, "Paisley," sharply and pulled her away to a corner to talk.

Parker's hands were in fists, but he didn't move. Esther crossed the room and put her hand on his shoulder, afraid he was going to do something he would regret.

"Don't, Parker. He's not worth it," Esther said.

"Yes, he is," Parker growled. "I don't need a peacemaker now. I need a baseball bat."

"Hardly," Sophie said. "Besides, you've got a hot date tonight. And it looks like Paisley can take care of herself, so stand down big brother."

Parker closed his eyes, and Esther let go of his shoulder and held his hand while she watched him struggle to relax. Finally, he opened his eyes.

"Let's get this over with." Parker let go of her hand and went back to help his father, who was trying to move the huge ladder.

"What did I miss?" Nephi came in carrying a couple cases of candy.

"Everything," Sophie said. "I'll fill you in while you help put up twinkle lights."

The doors opened again and Mr. Kelly, the principal, came in with Jackson and Bubba. "Ms. Priest, Nevaeh. Where should we put these two to work?"

Angelica Rose emerged from a pile of boxes near Ms. Priest's office. "They can help me with the refreshments. I need two strong men to set up tables and help me tape down extension cords for my chocolate fountain."

"Great," Principal Kelly said. "When you're done with that, boys, you can help me set up the televisions, projectors, and screens for the black and white movies."

Principal Kelly smiled and headed toward Ms. Priest's office. Esther was surprised to see Aiden Van Doren catch up to him and stand in front of him, blocking his way.

"I'm her man," Aiden said. He folded his arms across his chest. "You are an inappropriate coworker."

Principal Kelly's back was to Esther, but his body language was undeniably angry. He stepped closer to Aiden, one fist raised, and said something quietly. Esther only caught a few words. "Take you down . . . short . . ." Aiden smirked and pushed past the principal, who turned, giving Esther a glimpse of his angry red face. He strode to the doors and out of the library, leaving Esther to realize she'd been holding her breath.

River Peace must have been testing his fog machine. A bank of clouds gathered around Esther's feet and Aiden Van Doren began laughing like a giddy schoolboy.

"Is this fog going to hurt my books?" Ms. Priest asked.

"Now, honey," Aiden said, still chuckling.

Nevaeh dropped the bag she was carrying for her mother. Her eyes gathered like a storm. She frowned and locked eyes with Esther. She mouthed the word *jerk*, rolled her eyes, and said to her mom, "I'm going back out to the truck to bring the rest of the stuff in. Can Bubba help me after he is done with the tables?"

Before Nevaeh got to the door, both doors flew open. A small man in a green, greasy shirt and jeans burst into the room. He was bald, with random hairs sticking out of his head, eyebrows, and ears and a shaggy beard ringed the rest of his face. Every inch of his bald head was fire red, and his hands were clenched in fists.

"Dad?" Jackson said.

"Aiden Van Doren!" Jackson's dad bellowed. He marched through the fog and to the back of the room, where Aiden ducked behind River Peace's skinny body. Aiden's mouth was open, and his eyes were as round as glass bottle bottoms.

"Aiden! Don't you hide from me, you coward! How could you! Not one call! I said I'd pay you! That tow truck is my livelihood. How do you 'spect me to feed my boy!"

Aiden Van Doren's spray-tanned face became red. "You didn't make your payment!"

"I gave you what you wanted instead. You're not getting another thing from me. I don't care how much money you have. I'm going to kill you!" Mr. Green took two steps toward Aiden when Jackson bellowed at him.

"Dad!" Jackson screamed. His eyes were as round as Aiden's. He dropped a tray of caramel apples onto a nearby table, his mouth open in horror, and threw himself in front of his father. Both hands on his father's shoulders, he pushed against the little man who strained to get to Van Doren. "It's my fault, Dad. The check bounced. I made a mistake in my numbers."

Van Doren stopped short, fists raised. Ms. Priest ran to put her arm across Van Doren's heaving chest.

"You don't want me to go to the police about you, Green! You better take your son and your secrets out the door!" Aiden yelled over the top of Ms. Priest.

A look of confusion crossed Ms. Priest's face as her attention turned from Mr. Green to Aiden.

Principal Kelly came running and pulled Ms. Priest away. "I'm going to call the police!"

Jackson's dad looked like a rooster with his feathers on fire. "A man should never take another man's livelihood! Aiden! Man up. Maybe I should tell that scrawny thing you call a girlfriend why you call me regularly." He cackled. "Boy!" he yelled at Jackson. "You have some explaining to do." He turned on his heels and went out the double doors into the wind.

Jackson stood at the doors, watching him go.

"Esther."

Esther jumped when Ms. Priest said her name. She realized her heart was racing and her own fists were clenched. Anger rolled through her. It felt too much like her own childhood—her dad, her mom, the fights.

"Just sit down. Catch your breath," Ms. Priest said.

"I'd rather work."

"I need to check on Aiden and Jackson. Why don't you help Sophie and Mr. Stuart hang the twinkle lights on the ceiling? We have ten cases." She winked.

"Come on, Sophie." They walked toward the ladder where Parker was talking to his dad.

Esther said, "I'm sorry, Parker. Trouble follows Jackson. Paisley doesn't . . ." Parker cut Esther off before she could finish.

"You don't know what Jackson is dealing with, besides his father. I just talked to Dad. Don't judge him. He wouldn't share what he knew, but I trust my dad. He said to give Jackson a break. We didn't judge you and you didn't judge us." He shrugged and walked away. His remarks stung. Her heart dropped. *He's right. I sound like a judgmental gossip.* She felt tears welling up and turned her head, embarrassed.

"Well, I think he is a real piece of work, as your Grandma Mable would say. And a jerk! Don't you apologize for that one, Esther." Sophie slapped her on the back. "Men."

Esther couldn't help but laugh. "And what do you know about men, Sophie?"

"One word. Ransom Abrams. Okay, two words. And I'm doing more research. Today's data will be added to my journals."

Mr. Stuart brought a box of lights to Esther. "Come on, girls. We have a lot of work to do. Esther, why don't you go up the ladder and we'll hand the lights to you." Mr. Stuart handed her a small roll of wire, a box of tacks, and wire cutters.

Mr. Stuart froze. Esther followed his line of sight. He was staring at Jackson, who was talking to Ms. Priest and Aiden Van Doren.

"Excuse me for a minute, girls," Mr. Stuart said, and walked over to Jackson.

Esther watched Aiden go back to work with River. Mr. Stuart and Ms. Priest took Jackson into her small library office and closed the door. Principal Kelly let himself into the office and blocked Esther's view.

"Well, that happened." Sophie startled Esther.

"Yeah, but what was it," Esther said.

"Small towns. Got to love them," Sophie said and went back to work untangling lights.

Bubba Jones stood by the office with his arms folded, looking sullenly at the closed glass door.

"For a big guy who just threatened us on social media because he said he was protecting Jackson, Bubba sure didn't step in and help Jackson. I think he's all social media talk and no action," Esther said.

Sophie handed Esther some wire cutters. "Why don't you go up the ladder, Amazon woman, and I will hand you the lights. It looks like Parker's dad was poking tiny pieces of wire into the seams in the pressed tin and making hooks for the lights."

"Oh, yes." Esther's usually sharp brain was stuck watching Bubba, to see if he would get angry. Bubba spun around and glared at her. She shivered. *He must have felt me staring at him.* He left the library in long, angry strides.

Chapter Seven

The Fairy Grandmother

Parker and Nephi left the school earlier than Esther. Esther swung open the front door and took the stairs to her room at a dead run. They would be at her house in less than an hour to pick her and Sophie up.

The decorating had taken longer than anyone thought it would. She still hadn't found time to clear the air with Parker about judging Jackson and about how she felt about not being asked to the dance. *Even if we had time to talk, I am not sure why his assumption I would go with him bothered me so much. It so hard for me to trust anyone. I just need to relax.*

Hanging lights had been more difficult than they expected. She had spent the bulk of the day on a ladder hanging the strings of lights carefully, without damaging the antique pressed tin ceiling. It was a trick and by the end, she smelled like she had run a marathon. *If I can tell, so could everyone else in the room.*

She jumped in the shower, still wondering what she should do with her hair. She hadn't found anything at the thrift store. She and Sophie dug out their old Halloween costumes and tried to make the best of what they had. They finally decided to go as lady pirates. And after all, it was a costume ball, so any costume should work.

Her phone pinged.

Text from Sophie: *Did you see Brittney Belisar's costume online? She must have scrapped* Today's Teen Magazine *for something a little older.*

Sophie sent a screenshot. Brittney was dressed as an angel who forgot her dress. Her dress looked sheer and was covered in sequins.

Text to Sophie: *I think she has a flesh-colored leotard on.*
Text to Esther: *Gross! She should add some devil horns to that outfit.*

Esther looked at her brown dress laid out on the bed with its long leather vest, paper sword, and eye patch and groaned. *I guess this isn't junior high anymore. High school is the big leagues. Maybe I could cut it short and shred the hem? I would have to shave my legs. Crepes! Look at the time.*

Someone knocked on her door. "Not now, Mary. I have a major problem to solve." She was still in her robe, with her wet hair dripping on the floor.

"Esther, it's me. Open up. Sophie's here." Grandma Mable knocked again.

Esther unlocked the door and peeked through the opening.

"Surprise!" Sophie and Grandma Mable grinned like they had just won the lottery.

"Are you surprised? Please tell me you didn't know." Sophie pushed her way into the room carrying a bag with her. "Your Grandma asked me if we were ready for the ball, and I showed her our costumes. Then I showed her suggested costumes from the fashion editor in *Today's Teen Magazine.* Anyway, she ordered some dresses for us, and my mom and dad picked them up in Portland yesterday. I brought some things for our hair. I have glitter spray and . . ."

"I can't believe it . . ." Esther was stunned. "Grandma! Thank you." She fell into Grandma Mable's arms and gave her a tight hug.

"Whoa! I can't breathe. All I did was rent some costumes from the city. You still have to get the dress back in one piece or we own it."

"Thank you, thank you. A thousand times thank you."

"You haven't even tried them on." Mable laid the garment bags on the bed and unzipped one, chuckling softly.

"I ordered you both ball gowns or Cinderella sets."

"What if they don't fit?" Esther picked up the baby pink dress that was the larger of the two.

"The back panels are elastic, and they showed Sophie's mom how to use an inner elastic to tighten the waist if necessary. I think I can do it, and if not, she'll come over."

"Crowns!" Sophie held up a silver tiara triumphantly.

"Crowns?" Mary's voice traveled from her bedroom. She ran into Esther's room and jumped on the bed into the middle of the gowns and pirate gear.

Chapter Eight

May I Have This Dance?

Nephi, Paisley, Parker, Esther, and Sophie posed for photos on Esther's grand front porch. Sophie's mother and father were there snapping pictures. They brought both girls a hibiscus wrist corsage Sophie's Hawaiian grandmother had ordered for her to remind her she was loved. Papa J, Esther's mom, and Mable gushed while they snapped shots with everyone's cell phones. Mary, dressed in her own princess dress-up dress and photobombed almost every picture until Hart finally chased down the giggly mini monarch.

"I should have dressed as a chauffeur. I feel like a fifth wheel, literally," Sophie said.

"Sophie, you can be my other date." Paisley knelt slightly in her Regency era gown. "Sophie, would you do the honor of giving me the first dance on your dance card?"

Sophie pulled her chin in and bowed, "Ah, hem," she cleared her throat and in a deep voice said, "I'd be honored, m'lady."

"Hey, now!" Nephi pulled a tragically bent cardboard sword from the prince's suit Paisley had made him wear. "You, sir. I challenge you to a duel."

"Listen, fancy pants. Lower your weapon before I put a run in your pantyhose," Sophie said as she straightened out her tiara, pulled her dress up, and marched to the car.

Parker laughed so hard Esther thought he snorted. "Fair Lady, Esther, wilt thou come with me?" He held his arm out, and she put her hand gently on his elbow.

"It's hard to see in this mask." Esther's mask had pink and white feathers and covered the entire top of her face. "I keep getting feathers stuck in my tiara," she giggled. "But I love it. Thanks for making it, Paisley. I didn't know you were an artist."

"It's more of a craft. Mom and I are hard-core crafters. We set the attic up as a workroom. You should come see it. Personally, I love my mask." She touched hers. It was mint green like her dress and formed to fit her face. It also went up into two wings on either side of her eyes, and was covered in tiny white diamonds on the top half.

Parker had a suit that matched Nephi's, complete with black tights. But he wore his cowboy boots. The pointed shoes pinched his feet. The boots made him look comical.

"At least our masks are manly." Nephi took a selfie of his black felt mask and feathered hat. "We're going to need two cars to get your massive dresses to the school."

"Watch it, bub. No one calls me big," Sophie said. "Shotgun!"

Parker drove Esther and followed Nephi car. "You know he spent hours washing Papa J's Jeep for tonight." Esther smiled at Parker.

"E? I know things have been kind of tense this week and we haven't really had a chance to talk it out, but I was wondering . . ." Parker's voice trailed off as he made a turn and watched the road. He reached out and held her hand.

"I know. I'm sorry." Esther searched his face.

He glanced at her with sad eyes. "Can we just put Jackson and my blunder about asking you to the ball aside for tonight? We have something special planned for dinner after the dance."

"I'm sorry." She looked down at his hand and hers.

"Don't say that. You always say that. You don't have anything to be sorry about."

"Sorry," Esther said.

Parker chuckled and shook his head.

"What do you have planned?" Esther asked.

"It's a mystery." He winked at her.

The car jostled as it entered the west parking lot. Parker turned it off and got out. She was about to open her door when she realized he had come around and was opening it for her.

A truck turned into the parking lot, its lights temporarily blinding her. She closed her eyes until she heard its diesel motor stop. She peeked. The truck was parked under a streetlamp. Its headlights turned off.

"Isn't that Jackson's dad? He has his tow truck back." Esther pointed at the truck parked in its favorite place, waiting for a high schooler's car to need a tow. Two boys from her class walked over and Mr. Green rolled down the window and was talking to them.

Parker interrupted her thoughts, smiled, winked, and held out his hand to her. "M'lady. It's another mystery." She took his hand while she used her other hand to collect mountains of her taffeta gown. "Are you in there, m'lady?"

"Sir. Surely you jest." She chuckled and straightened her tiara one more time. Then, taking his hand, they mounted the old stone steps and entered the ball behind their friends.

It was already getting crowded. There must have been a hundred students or a third of the school's student body in the library. Everyone had a variety of costumes on. Some had masks, some didn't. Some danced while others were laughing and talking.

The music was thumping. Aiden Van Doren was dressed as Zorro and eating out of a bag of candy. River Peace was dressed as himself, a throwback from the seventies. Except he had one of the paper mask invitations tied to his face. Esther chuckled when she realized the mask still had the popsicle stick attached.

The white lights reflected on the high tin ceiling as they twinkled, making it appear as if the night sky was above them. The fog machine had laid down a light layer across the floor that dissipated in front of the fireplace, which was burning brightly. Black and white movies played on various screens.

"Look at the fire!" Esther was giddy. "I've never seen it like this. It's wonderful."

Nephi, Paisley, and Sophie were gathered around the warm flames and waved at Esther and Parker, who joined them.

The fireplace was welcoming. Gold candelabras were on the mantle, with autumn leaves spread across the stone. Electric candles were grouped on all the tables with donated pumpkins, branches, yellow and orange flowers, and dried autumn leaves. Everything made the room look like a magical autumn garden. In different places in the room, they had grouped bare branches that looked like trees. They were decorated with white lights and sunflowers, and pumpkins surrounded the trunks, hiding the Christmas tree stands.

Near the library office and door to the hallway and kitchen was a long table set with ornate iron candelabras with electric tapers flickering in the dark. The table had a red velvet tablecloth and thirty or forty silver trays at different levels.

"Nevaeh's mom is amazing," Esther said over the music. The volume was loud enough it was hard to talk. They were playing "Masquerade" from *The Phantom of the Opera* soundtrack.

The west doors burst open and like a queen entering a ballroom, Madison Merriweather made a grand entrance dressed as a witch. A somber-looking Bridget Merriweather looked stunning. She was dressed as a magical student from her mother's book, *Blessed Be*. She lit up when she saw Paisley, Esther, and Sophie. Esther saw her say something to her mother, then wander away as a sudden swarm of groupies surrounded their favorite author.

Bridget smiled broadly, put her arms out, and ran to hug Paisley. She gave Esther and Sophie a hug, and then Parker. "I am so glad you are all here!" Bridget shouted over the music. She tapped Parker on the shoulder. "Parker, dance with me!"

"Dance with us!" Paisley took her hand. Paisley, Nephi, and Bridget danced into the crowd on the dance floor, laughing and spinning to the music.

"I wish I could dance like that," Esther said.

"I'll just hold up this wall." Sophie leaned against the black oak wall.

Between songs, Parker returned. "Come on guys. I'm starving." Parker rubbed his belly. "Let's go say hello to Ms. Priest and see if we can eat all the refreshments." Parker smiled at Esther and Sophie, who followed him through the crowd toward the food.

Angelica brought out a tray of caramel apples sprinkled in something that looked like tiny diamonds. She put them on the furthest end of the table.

"Oh!" Ms. Priest clapped her hands. She was, of course, dressed like a witch, in a deep purple gown and robe. She had a cauldron of bubbling root beer in front of her. Dry ice floating on the top. "Those are gorgeous! How did you make them?"

"Kids love these," Angelica said. She glowed. There were four or five trays of caramel apples.

Angelica was dressed as the queen of hearts. Her gown looked like a playing card from *Alice in Wonderland*. "The diamonds are rock candy." She handed a sparkling apple to Ms. Priest. "Try one."

"Thank you!" she said loudly over the music. "I'll eat it in a few minutes. I want to make sure the root beer is ready to go." She took a large wooden paddle and stirred the cauldron, making fog from the dry ice spill over the sides and onto the floor.

Angelica smiled. Then Esther watched her expression change. Her face went flat, and frowned. She rolled her eyes and left the room through the double doors that led to the hall and kitchen. Esther turned around and followed her line of sight to Nevaeh.

Nevaeh was making her way through the students on the dance floor. She was dressed in rainbow pants and a rainbow shirt with a gold horn tied to her head. A broad grin split her face. When she reached the candy bar, she took a candy bag and started eating.

"What are you?" Parker asked.

"I am a rainbow unicorn." She posed like a prancing horse, and Esther burst into laughter.

"Girls." Parker shook his head.

"Parker!" Esther scolded him and shrugged at Nevaeh.

Parker took a chocolate and ate it while Esther scowled at him.

Madison Merriweather was being followed by a few girls dressed as white witches from her recent bestselling book *Solstice*. She joined Ms. Priest behind the table. "Angelica has outdone herself! I am going to put this wonderful candy bar in my next book. It's a work of art! Now. What can I do to help?"

"Keep the kids back until we are ready to serve the food!" Ms. Priest laughed musically.

"No problem. We shall use our magic wands to turn them into frogs if they approach. Right, girls?" Madison waved a glittering silver wand, and her groupies giggled. "Girls, turn Parker into a newt."

Jackson Green and Bubba Jones had dressed as themselves. They slid past Madison and began pocketing bags of candy off the table.

"Halt, knave!" Madison said. She laughed heartily.

Bubba sneered at her and ignored the request.

I can't believe them. What is wrong with those two? They'll eating all the refreshments.

"We aren't ready to serve." Sophie took a caramel apple out of Bubba's hands.

"Hey! I'm eating that. What is your problem, shorty?" Bubba laughed, and Jackson stepped in between them.

"You!" Sophie said and threw Bubba's apple away.

"We're hungry," Jackson said.

"Me too,"

"All right, boys. Show Ms. Merriweather some respect and wait until we're ready," Ms. Priest said. Carefully, she unwrapped another block of dry ice and dropped it into the plastic cauldron of root beer.

Principal Kelly emerged from the shadows. Jackson and Bubba quickly stepped back into the crowd.

Angelica turned on Christmas lights hidden under a sheer silver table runner. They twinkled through the gauzy fabric on top of the velvet tablecloth. She placed three more trays of dipped chocolates on the table. Small plates and napkins were stacked at one end.

Aiden Van Doren came through a crowd of kids lining up at the dessert table. "Cynnomon, is the food ready? Can I let the kids know refreshments are available?"

Ms. Priest looked at Angelica, who smiled and nodded before leaving to go back to the kitchen.

Handing Aiden the caramel apple encrusted in diamond rock candy, Ms. Priest said, "We're ready! Send the hordes to dine."

Aiden, now Zorro, held out the caramel apple like a sword. Cynnomon laughed coyly. He did a sweeping bow and took a large bite of the caramel apple, making Cynnomon Priest laugh harder.

He returned to the sound equipment and with his mouth still full, paused the music and said, "You may dine on sweets and treats compliments of Angelica Rose and the Sweet Treat Shops."

Esther looked around for Angelica, but she wasn't in the room. Aiden laughed a maniacal laugh, and the music started again.

"May I have this dance?" Parker asked.

"Esther, can you give me a hand with the root beer?" Ms. Priest was overrun with students.

Esther smiled at Parker and shrugged.

"Fine. I guess it's just me and Sophie." He picked up one of the sparkling caramel apples, gave her a huge smile, and melted into the chaos.

Esther grabbed a ladle and began filling cups while Ms. Priest kept loading candy bags on the quickly emptying table. Principal Kelly stood close to Ms. Priest monitoring kids going through the line. Angelica Rose returned with more chocolates for the refreshment table. Nevaeh followed her carrying a tray of caramel apples covered in candy corn.

Ms. Priest had stopped smiling. Principal Kelly was staring at her, but she was ignoring him.

"Here, Ms. Priest," Esther reached out for the ladle. "Take a break." She let Esther take over and melted into the crowd. Principal Kelly followed her.

Papa J and Esther's mom, Grace, came into the library from the hall doors. Her mother was wearing her rejected pirate outfit. Hart was dressed in a matching outfit. They joined her behind the table.

"Who are you supposed to be?" Esther yelled over the chaos.

"I am the Dread Pirate Roberts—from *The Princess Bride*, you know, the movie," Papa J said.

"And he is so handsome, my eye hurts." Her mother patted his face.

"Stop that rhyming. I mean it." Papa J grinned, proud of himself. Esther rolled her eyes.

"We'll take over so you can dance with your handsome prince," her mother shouted over the music.

"Thanks!" Esther handed her the ladle. She was looking for Parker when the music stopped, and she heard Nevaeh screaming.

"Help! Help! Help!" Nevaeh kept calling over and over.

"I'm going to faint . . ." Madison screamed and swayed. Bridget led her mother to a chair giving Esther full view of Aiden Van Doren's body on the dance floor twitching, making a bizarre face with bluish lips.

River Peace tapped the mic and said to the now silent onlookers, "Give him some room. Let him breathe people. Everything is fine."

"Help!" Nevaeh shrieked. People finally jumped into action.

"Hello, we need an ambulance," Sophie said into her phone.

Mrs. Stuart and Mr. Stuart were pushing their way through the shocked crowd toward the body. Esther closed the distance between her and Aiden Van Doren just in time to watch him throw up all over River Peace's sandals.

Mr. Stuart, a doctor, ran to Aiden's side and dropped to his knees and shook him, "Mr. Van Doren! Aiden! Stay with us!" He pulled up an eyelid. His pupils were constricted, his skin was pale and sweaty. His breathing seemed thready, shallow.

Angelica pushed through people to Mr. Stuart's side. "I used to be a nurse."

Mr. Stuart put his ear down to Van Doren's mouth and listened. He searched for his pulse on his neck and loosened the buttons on his shirt. Esther could hear the sirens. The ambulance was coming.

Angelica looked up and around the crowd. "Mr. Kelly! Do you have an AED? You know, a defibrillator?"

The principal looked confused.

Ms. Priest said, "Yes! I'll go get it." She pushed her way through the crowd toward the doors.

"Wait!" Mr. Stuart shouted at Ms. Priest. "The ambulance is already here." He began pumping on Aiden's chest and counting.

Principal Kelly ran to the doors and propped them open for the medics.

Ms. Priest stopped and came back to the scene, kneeling next to Aiden and touching his hand. Angelica looked at Ms. Priest with an odd mixture of anger and confusion, her eyes drawn together and frowning, hands fisted. Angelica pushed through the crowd and away from Aiden and Ms. Priest.

Dr. Stuart straightened Aiden's neck and was checking his pulse again when the medics pushed through the library door, carrying equipment.

"Get the gurney," one medic shouted to a third member of the ambulance team. He took over CPR for Dr. Stuart.

Ironpot came in behind them and pushed Esther and the crowd back so they could work on their patient. "Make way for the gurney!"

The students parted, mouths opened, some crying openly. Another medic with a gurney ran through the crowd and helped the other two lift Aiden. They ran for the door, pushing the gurney and carrying equipment.

The sound of the siren diminished after it left the parking lot. Ironpot looked at Esther and nodded before heading to the door to leave. Esther realized that Sophie was standing next to her. She reached out and they held hands. Parker put his arm around her. She began to shake uncontrollably.

"I think I am going to puke," Parker said. He dropped a candy bag, and taffy went everywhere.

Horrified, eyes wide, Esther swung around and began feeling his forehead.

He pushed her hand off, but he didn't look right. "I'm fine . . ." He slurred his words. Sophie's mouth fell open and her hands flew up to cover it as she stifled a scream.

"Sophie, stop Ironpot. We need another ambulance." Esther felt Parker's face. He had broken out into a cold sweat. His pupils were pinpoints despite the darkened room. He swayed slightly. "Nephi, Papa J!" she screamed for help.

Parker's knees buckled, and they both went down.

"No!" Esther screamed, falling on him. He was breathing. He looked at her and laughed.

Mrs. Stuart, Paisley, and Mr. Stuart crowded around him. Esther heard Mrs. Stuart wail and watched Paisley kneel next to her father, who was checking Parker's pulse.

"Parker! Parker!" Paisley's cries mixed with her mother's and the sound of a second ambulance. Everything seemed to go in slow motion for Esther. She kissed Parker's cold forehead and held his hand, feeling his faint pulse, while he laughed at a joke no one could hear.

"Parker. Talk to me." His father held his face in his hands. Parker laughed again, and then he threw up on his mother. She didn't care. He muttered something.

"Stand him up." His father and Paisley tried to pull him up. "We should keep him awake and moving." The door burst open, and another gurney and crew came in.

Esther stepped back. Her mother and Papa J surrounded her and Sophie. Nephi tried to follow the gurney out, but Ironpot stopped him. Parker's family left with the ambulance. Suddenly it was silent.

Blood pumping in her ears, shaking uncontrollably, Esther said weakly, "Parker . . ."

Ironpot held his hands up. "Everyone stay put. If you have been eating, put the food down. It is probably just a case of food poisoning."

"Excuse me!" Angelica Rose pushed past Esther. "I am sure the food is fine. I made most of it myself and supervised all the preparations."

Ironpot cocked his head at the small but loud woman. "Everyone, sit down!" He barked, and she did in the nearest chair. "Put your food down and sit down! Hart!"

"Right here!" Papa J called from the crowd and pushed his way toward Ironpot.

A girl somewhere in the room began to wail. Ironpot's eyes got big as the fear and confusion spread through the room. Kids were calling parents. Esther watched as girls started crying on their boyfriends' shoulders, and Nevaeh was standing facing the door, stunned, not moving.

"Esther," her mother said softly. "Esther, Sophie." She said it firmly this time. "Come with me. She pulled Esther and Sophie toward the library office. Nephi and Papa J followed them. Esther realized that Ms. Priest was standing alone, still holding a ladle, and openly weeping. Cynnomon Priest fell into Esther's mother's arms. Then her mother swept her into the library office and shut the door. Papa J let himself into the room, leaving Esther alone with Sophie and Nephi. Esther was shaking so hard her teeth chattered.

Jackson Green passed Esther, and Bubba followed him. They went out the door to the hallway.

"No doubt Jackson and Bubba are just walking out again, while we all wait for the police to give us directions." Sophie folded her arms, pursed her lips, and kicked the table leg hard enough to make the root beer slosh.

Text to Parker from Esther: *Are you there? Parker? I'm scared.*

Esther and Sophie sat behind the library desk outside Ms. Priest's office door. Esther stared at the blank screen on her phone. No reply. Every part of her felt numb.

"Snap out of it. Esther!" Sophie touched Esther's shoulder.

Like surfacing from deep water, Esther looked up.

Sophie wasn't wearing her glasses. The tiara was off, and her mask was pushed up on her forehead, exposing her angry eyes, drawn together in the center. She frowned, hands on hips. "Listen, E. Parker needs us. I don't think Ironpot's right. This is not food poisoning. I think it's just plain poison. And I am betting it's the boys that just left the building. Ironpot is gone, and Papa J is working with the chief to interview people. We're the only eyes they've got."

"I . . . we were going to talk. Things were kind of . . ." *This is the story of my life. Unfinished relationships blown to smithereens. Sophie shouldn't have gotten on him about asking me. It's a stupid dance. I don't care if I don't go to another one.*

As if she had heard her thoughts, Sophie put her hands on her shoulders and shook her. "E! Please. Don't be upset with me about making him ask you. Are you feeling okay? Where's my fierce E? Get mad!"

"Are you a mind reader?" Esther stood, towering over Sophie's short body.

"No, but I know you. I'm sorry I pushed him to ask you and I'll apologize for listening to that rag of a magazine when he's better." Sophie folded her arms, looking intensely into Esther's eyes.

"Do you think he will get better? What if . . ." Her heart dropped. *I don't even know if he's alive.* Feeling a rush of blood pumping in her ears, she put her hand on her chest as if that would slow her heart down and tried to put her head between her knees. She felt faint.

"Do you know what's odd?" Sophie said.

"Everything?"

Sophie smiled. "True. But don't you think it's odd that we were just talking to Nevaeh about death and that she said everyone dies around her?"

"You're right. I've been so focused on Parker, I haven't really paid much attention to Nevaeh."

"Maybe we should." Sophie raised one eyebrow. "Maybe we should find out exactly how her dad and her stepdad died?"

"You mean Nevaeh may be responsible?" Esther scanned the room, looking for her Nevaeh. She was sitting by the fireplace near Angelica, but talking to Esther's mother.

"Hey! You! Walking stomach! Get away from that food!" Sophie marched over to Nephi. He stood looking at the table. He turned and faced her. His face was pale, shaken, and his eyes looked like they could overflow any moment.

"I wasn't going to eat it. I . . . I can't remember what Parker ate." He shook his head and went back to studying the long table with trays of caramel apples, bags of taffy, bowls of candy corn and nuts, and a cauldron of root beer going flat. "How do we know it's even the food?"

Sophie's arms dropped. She did something Esther had never seen her do before. She reached up with her small arms and hugged his massive form. "Sorry. I'm so glad it wasn't you or Esther."

Closing his eyes, Nephi reached down and patted her back until she let go. He said softly, "Does it matter? It's Parker. He is our best friend. He loves you, Sophie."

Esther joined them. She searched the table as if whatever the problem was would present itself.

Sophie looked over her shoulder and grabbed a handful of taffy and put it in her pocket. "Nephi, find a bag. I want a caramel apple."

"Soph, what are you thinking?" Esther asked.

"No one is better at solving mysteries than we are. My parents are scientists. We have a lab. I want to look at this food. I don't trust the police. Ironpot is gone and I don't know the officer over there."

"Which one?" Esther asked.

"The one who looks older than Grandma Mable. I think his name is Dickerson." Nephi pointed at the west door to the library. An officer stood in front of the door, while the kids tried to talk him into letting them leave. He was about Esther's height and as round as he was tall.

His hands rested on his duty belt. While Esther watched, he removed his hat, straightened his gray hair, and moved a chair over and sat by the door.

Esther went to the library counter and pulled out a pen. She went back to Sophie and Nephi. Using paper from the printer behind the counter, they began writing down the names of the people in the room now and of everyone who had already left, like Bubba and Jackson. Principal Kelly was sitting by the door to the parking lot talking to a parent who was trying to come in.

"It's a good thing this is a small town and there's only about a hundred students here," Esther said. "Remember what Grandma Mable taught us? Follow the money. Do you think it could be one of the kids? Or is it something else? Van Doren has a lot of money."

"Had," Sophie corrected her.

"Are we sure he's dead? He could still be alive." Shaking her head, Esther turned to a new page. She wrote Van Doren's name at the top.

"You better add Parker's name. Where's Grace and Hart by the way?" Nephi scanned the room. "There's your mom."

"Parker's not dead," Esther said, her mouth falling open with the realization that she had no clue.

"Let's go see if we can help your mom," Sophie said.

Esther followed Sophie and Nephi to the fireplace. Esther's mother was sitting on a couch with Nevaeh, who was sobbing and holding a pile of party napkins. "Sophie," Esther whispered before they reached them. "Look at Ms. Rose."

Nevaeh's mother, Angelica Rose, sat on another couch, her arms folded, frowning. Madison Merriweather was on the same couch. Madison was looking sympathetically at Nevaeh and talking softly to Angelica Rose. "This must be so hard on Nevaeh."

Angelica turned to Madison. "On Nevaeh? I suppose so. She can be a little dramatic, but you're right. I should be paying more attention to how this is affecting her. I was just so in love with Aiden. I keep replaying the last things we said to each other." Angelica stifled a sob, folded her arms and turned her back on Madison, blowing her nose.

"Wow. Grace is taking more care of Nevaeh than her mother," Nephi said.

Esther stopped, pulled Nephi, and then Sophie back. Quietly, she said to Nephi, "She isn't Nevaeh's mom. She actually adopted Nevaeh after her mom and dad died. She was her nanny."

"And right now, for an adoptive mom, she seems cold." Sophie rolled her eyes.

"All I know is Nevaeh needs us. Everyone responds to trauma differently," Nephi said. Ever practical, Nephi joined Esther's mom by the fire. He took a chair with him and sat looking at Nevaeh, blocking Angelica Rose's view.

Nevaeh looked at him, still sobbing and gulping while she talked. "I was mad at him, but I didn't hate him. What if he dies? I said terrible things."

"Mr. Van Doren?" Nephi asked.

Esther's mom reached out and Nevaeh fell into her arms, crying on her shoulder. "It isn't your fault." Nevaeh nodded and blew her nose.

"Well, I'm furious. How dare they think it's my candy?" Jumping to her feet, Angelica brushed Sophie's shoulder hard as she passed her on the way back to the kitchen. She snatched a tray of caramel apples and took them with her.

The officer by the door saw her leave with the tray. "Hey! Put that down." He pointed at Angelica who was trotting to the doors.

Angelica went out the hall door followed by the officer and Esther. Esther looked back, just in time to see a dozen kids rush the door and scatter in various directions down the dark hallways.

"Hey!" Officer Dickerson said. Papa J poked his head out of the door to the teacher's lounge. Angelica ignored them both and kept going.

"Stop or I'll taser you!" Dickerson shouted.

That did it. Angelica dropped the whole tray onto the floor, apples sticking with a sickening thud, and put her hands up in the air.

Esther watched in fascination as Ms. Rose turned to face them.

"I'm just cleaning up."

"Go back into the library and wait for Detective Kohornen." The officer left the tray and apples on the floor and turned around, almost running into Esther. "You too!"

"Esther. Stay with your mom. I'll be there in a minute." Esther looked back at Papa J and saw a tearful Ms. Priest standing next to him. Angelica Rose stomped past her and went back into the library.

Sophie met Esther at the door. "Did you bring a purse?"

"No. Why?"

She pulled a sticky apple wrapped in a napkin out of the folds of her gown and then quickly tucked it back in.

Esther thought for a minute. "The library return box. I have a key. Quick."

They tried casually heading for the desk, when the older officer said, "Go sit down."

"I have to get my purse. You know. Girl stuff." Sophie shrugged. The officer turned red and stalked away.

They were locking the apple in the return box built into the library counter when Detective Kohornen and Officer Neilson, Ms. Priest's father, came into the library through the west door dragging a few of the runaway kids back into the room.

"Listen Up! Everyone! Stop touching things and line up at the door!" Korhonen's round face was bright red, and he frowned when he was finished bellowing at them. He started giving the officers directions.

"We can't leave yet," Sophie said. "We have to gather clues, something, anything we can find. We helped with the dance. Maybe they will let us stay as part of the decoration committee."

"Esther," her mother said. She waved her over to the fireplace. Nevaeh got up and followed Angelica Rose toward the officers at the door. "Esther."

Esther waved and wove her way through students to her mother with Nephi and Sophie.

"Where's Hart?" her mother asked.

"Last time I saw him, he was talking to Ms. Priest in the teacher's lounge."

"Stay here." Her mom went out the double doors to the hall.

"You kids! Over here. Esther," A tall, but lanky officer called.

"Crepes, it's officer Davids. He's nice, but I don't want him pushing us out." Sophie waved weakly at the officer. "Officer Davids," she called. "We're just finding our parents." She pushed Esther and Nephi in the direction of the double doors.

In the hallway, they ran into Papa J and her mom talking to Ms. Priest. She was crying and Esther's mom had her arm around her shoulder. The adults all stopped talking as they got closer.

"Is Kohornen here?" Papa J asked.

Esther nodded. He passed her, heading back into the room.

"Ms. Priest? I don't know if it helps, but your dad, Officer Neilson, is here," Esther said softly.

Ms. Priest smiled weakly, tears and makeup running down her face.

Papa J came back out into the hallway. "Cynnomon, your dad said he loves you and will talk to you as soon as he can. As for the rest of us—Kohornen wants to talk to Ms. Priest, as well as everyone who helped with refreshments before we leave."

The officers took kids' names, looked at IDs, and gathered their contact information. Parents were lined up in the parking lot picking kids up. Even kids that drove had parents waiting for them. They asked the students for the names of their friends who had left the dance before the police arrived.

Madison and Bridget were among the first to leave. Esther worried about Madison. She looked positively wrecked. Her makeup and hair had wilted. She seemed to be having a hard time standing, and when she did, she shook uncontrollably. Holding her mother's arm, Bridget had pushed to the front of the line. "I'm taking my mom to urgent care to be checked out."

The officers took their information and let them go quickly, not wanting another patient on their hands.

I wonder if there's news. Word spreads fast in Necanicum. Esther checked her phone again. Nothing. Social media was also eerily silent.

Desperate and terrified, Esther started to text Parker yearning for an answer, his voice: *Talk to me. I'm worried.* Then she deleted it and wrote, *I am so afraid.* She sent the raw, honest truth, wanting to believe in miracles, but afraid to hope.

A little bubble popped up. She held her breath, waiting for the text to come through.

Text from Parker's phone to Esther: *This is Paisley. Pray! He has been intubated. He stopped breathing on his own. He is unconscious. We are waiting until they let us see him. They are still working on him in the emergency room. They want to know what made him sick. No one is sure. They asked if he did drugs. Pray hard.*

Esther felt the world spin around her. Her heart dropped and tears started falling uncontrollably. Her hands shook, and she covered her mouth so a scream wouldn't escape.

Sophie surprised her by taking her phone out of her hand and reading the text. She hugged Esther while handing the phone to Nephi.

"God help him," Nephi said. He gave the phone to Esther's mom. His hands were in fists. He looked at Esther, glaring under gathered brows. "I am going to kill someone."

"Hasn't there been enough of that tonight," Grace said. "I understand why you're angry, but don't do anything you'll regret. We don't know what happened yet."

"Yes, we do," Nephi growled.

"What do you mean?" Papa J asked.

"You know it too. Jackson and Bubba were there when we made the candy. They were mad at me. Maybe they did something dumb. They said they would and where are they now," Nephi spoke through clenched teeth.

"Hart?" Grace said. "Can we just give them our information and get these kids out of here?"

"We can't go yet, Mom." Esther held up her hands in protest. "We have to find what made him sick. They need it to help him."

Kohornen left the chaos at the door and made his way to their group. "Hart. We need to talk." He motioned and Papa J followed him. So did everyone's eyes.

Esther, Sophie, and Nephi watched them whisper by the refreshments. Officer Neilson stopped long enough to give Ms. Priest a short hug and say how glad he was that she was okay before Detective Kohornen called his name and put him back to work.

Then the detective made a sweeping motion. Papa J shook his head and folded his arms, looking down. He looked back at Ms. Priest and then they talked for a minute more.

"I have got to learn to read lips." Sophie held up her cell phone and began taking random pictures of the room. Esther turned hers to video and ran it around the room.

Principal Kelly was talking to the janitor, Simon. Simon nodded and Esther filmed Principal Kelly walking to the exit.

"Hey, you kids!" Kahornen came toward Esther with his hand out. "Give me your cell phone."

Esther stuck hers down the front of her dress.

"Esther!" Her mother's mouth was open, and she was clearly shocked.

"Young lady, you give me that cell." Kahornen stood in front of her holding his hand out, his red cheeks even brighter if that were possible. "This is a crime scene."

"Fine. She will erase it. We promise." Sophie stepped between Esther and the detective, her fingers crossed behind her back.

"Sophie." Papa J shook his head. "I'll make sure she erases it, Kohornen."

"If I so much as see one picture on social media from your phones, I will get a subpoena and take them for good." Kohornen turned to Ms. Priest. "Ms. Priest? Cynnomon Priest?"

"Yes? You know me, detective." Ms. Priest's purple witch's dress had new stains on the front, her hat was askew, and any makeup she had on was smeared or gone. *She is so pale.*

"We would like you to come to the station with us for an interview."

"Can my dad or Hart come with me?" Her voice shook, and she turned her large moist eyes in Hart's direction.

"No. Officer Neilson is working. This isn't a social call. You need to come with us, or we will take you in." Kohornen pulled out his car keys. It was clear the conversation was over. "Davids, find those boys."

"Yes, sir." Davids, who was talking to River Peace, nodded.

"And Davids," Kohornen closed his eyes and rubbed his face in exasperation, "Mr. Peace may not touch his equipment. What part of don't touch anything do you people not understand?"

"You're interfering with my rights, man," River Peace said. He pulled out a small cigarette and tried to light it. Officer Davids ran across the room and snatched it out of his hands. "Hey, it's legal."

"That's it. Davids!" Kohornen's gloves were off. He took Ms. Priest by the elbow and dragged her toward the door. Neilson held the door open, his eyes glued to his daughter.

Kohornen, still holding Ms. Priest's elbow, turned around and bellowed, "Get everyone's names and get them out of here. I want contact information. And no purses, backpacks, or bags leave the room. They can take their ID and cash. That's it! In the name of all that is holy!" And with that, he blew through the west doors into the night with Ms. Priest.

Esther watched Neilson follow Ms. Priest until Kohornen had her in his car. The library doors swung closed. She reached up and touched her face and realized it was wet with tears.

"Come on," Papa J said. "Let's get out of here."

"Shouldn't we collect more evidence?" Sophie looked around the room frantically.

"Sophie," Papa J said softly. Everyone looked at him. "Do not make a sound. Don't react and don't repeat this." He had their little group's full attention. He said softly under his breath, "Aiden Van Doren was declared dead on arrival. This is now the scene of a murder."

Chapter Nine

Is This the Last Dance?

The house was quiet. Esther and Sophie washed their makeup off and were making up the trundle bed for Sophie when Esther's mom knocked on their door.

"Come in."

The door opened a crack, and Esther's mom poked her head in. "I got a text from the detective. He wants to make sure you deleted your video."

"Of course I did." Esther started unplugging her phone from the charger to show her mother.

"I trust you. I just had to make sure. Listen, I am sorry I was so busy with Nevaeh. How are you two doing?"

"You know us. We're always great." Sophie smiled at her.

"I do know you. That's why I'm asking. Listen, I know you both love a mystery, but this time things are really dangerous. How about just trusting Papa J and the police to do their job?"

"You're probably right, Mom," Esther smiled. "Night. Love you."

Her mom smiled. "I knew I could count on you. You're a good girl, E. You both are. I texted the Stuarts. They said Paisley was keeping you updated, and that Parker is in the best care possible. Can I do anything to help?"

Holding her boiling emotions deep inside, Esther shook her head, no.

Her mother gave her a gentle hug and kissed her forehead. She held Esther's face in her hands and studied her eyes. Esther closed them and tried not to cry. "I love you, Esther. I am grateful neither of you was hurt today." She gave her one more hug and paused at the door. "Parker is strong. I have a feeling everything will be okay.

What if it's not?

"Well . . . good night. See you in the morning."

"Night," Sophie said.

After closing the door, Esther picked up her garbage can and hugged it to her chest, sure she was going to throw up. She crawled into bed and held the can in her lap. Tears started to fall. "How can she know? We have to do something, Sophie."

"Did you really delete the video?" Sophie asked.

"Right after I sent it to you by email." She gave Sophie a small smile. Molly jumped from the desk onto her bed and tried to get between her and the garbage can.

"I wish we could go up to the hospital." Sophie climbed in between the blankets on her bed. Esther turned off her bedside lamp and let her eyes adjust to the light of the moon.

She put the can next to the bed and tried to stop crying.

"It's okay to cry. It's very healthy." Sophie turned on her side and looked at Esther.

Esther closed her eyes. Her chest heaved, and she cried quietly. Unable to stop, she gave in to her emotions and let salty tears run down her face, until all she could do was gasp for air. Finally, she took a deep, jagged breath and tried to blow it out slowly. When her breathing slowed, she looked back at Sophie.

Sophie reached out and held her hand silently.

"Sophie, the last time Parker and I really talked, I . . . it was . . . I was awful. He's never done anything to hurt me, and he was asking me why I didn't trust him." The words came tumbling out between jagged sobs. "You were right. He didn't ask me, but we had an understanding, you know? I don't care if he never asks me to do another thing, as long as I get to see him, and tell him I'm sorry."

"What do you have to be sorry for?" Sophie asked.

"Why didn't I trust him? What's wrong with me? I feel so broken sometimes." Esther took a tissue off the bedside and blew her nose loudly.

"You aren't broken. Bruised maybe. But you're stronger than you think. You just have this wall around you," Sophie said. She bit her lip like she did when she was thinking and went to push up her glasses, but they weren't there. "You know that song Grandma Mable plays over and over again about the wall? Take down the wall?"

Esther let out a strangled giggle. "I hate that song."

"Right? Well, I've examined it and it seems the person who wrote it built the wall to stay safe, but it just made him miserable. So, he had to take it down."

"He's worth the risk," Esther said softly. She closed her eyes and ran her fingers through her hair, making it stick up wildly. She blew her nose again. Gradually, her breathing slowed.

"Don't tell him I said this, okay? But he's pretty great. I'm sure he'll be okay. He's strong," Sophie said.

After a few minutes of silence, Esther checked her phone. "I haven't heard any more from Paisley. Do you think I should text her? It's all I can think about."

"Maybe he's sleeping. Maybe everything is okay, and she won't have any more news until he wakes up."

"I hope so." Her heart actually ached. It was a very real, very physical pain. "Good people always die young." Molly pawed at Esther's pile of thick hair and climbed on her hip to see Sophie.

"He isn't perfect, and you're definitely trouble," Sophie said.

Even in the dark, Esther could see Sophie's half smile and knew she was trying to comfort her in her very Sophie way. "Where should we start? Do you think they've figured out what killed Aiden?"

"I doubt it," Sophie said. "Autopsies done the same day someone dies only happen in the movies. Besides, in Coho County we only have one medical examiner."

"How can they help Parker if they don't know what it is?" Esther gathered her cat in her arms.

"I don't know, but I have the food samples I managed to sneak out in my dress. They're hidden in the garage fridge in a box marked *Sophie's—eat and die*. If they don't solve it, we will. I think we should start where Kohornen is starting. We know where Jackson Green and Bubba Jones live. If they didn't do it, maybe they saw something that might help."

"Do you think they did it and meant to kill someone?"

"I don't know. But we do know Jackson likes Paisley. Why risk hurting her twin, or worse, hurting her? Jackson and Bubba are always sneaking around. Even if Jackson or Bubba didn't do it, maybe they saw something?"

"I want to start at the hospital first thing in the morning. Would you walk up there with me? After we see Parker, we can walk to the trailer park. It isn't far."

"Absolutely. Should we ask Nephi if he wants to go? He could drive us."

"Only if he's up. I don't want to wait for him."

Esther's phone vibrated, and she jumped up.

Text from Bridget to Esther: *People are so mean. Did you see the social media post Maxine posted tonight?*
Text to Bridget: *No! Looking.*

"Sophie, it's hit social media."

Sophie rummaged for her phone. "If kids are posting pictures, there might be a clue in one of them. Something."

Esther opened social media and found the post. She sat back down on the side of the bed and let Miss Molly rub against her back and knead her with her paws. "Listen to this. Maxine Brandt says, 'We all know Jackson and Bubba did this and then scurried back under the rock they crawled out from under. They do things. All the things. They threatened, and we didn't listen. Maybe if the police actually listened to kids, this wouldn't have happened.' She posted photos, Sophie."

Esther closed her eyes and tried to slow her pounding heart. "Look," was all she got out before she ran to the bathroom and threw up. The photo was of her bent over Parker and his strange face. He looked awful. There were other photos. Even a photo of Maxine taking a selfie with Aiden Van Doren's dying body in the background.

Looking at the photos made Esther feel like she was having an out-of-body experience. When she returned to the room she said, "Who does that? Who takes a selfie when someone is in so much pain?"

"Everyone," Sophie answered. "It made Channel Ten's breaking news. 'Man dies and student sick after dance. Recent threats were made by two angry students to burn the school down. This may not be the threatened fire, but it still burns. Where was school leadership? Principal Kelly declined to make a statement.'" She showed Esther the news photo of Principal Kelly holding a hand up to cover his face. He was in the school parking lot by Jackson's father's truck. The parking lot was empty, except for the two men.

Esther closed her eyes. Sophie kept scrolling.

"I can't believe it. Listen to this garbage. National News says, 'Bestselling author Madison Merriweather risks life chaperoning high school event where violence takes place.'"

"What does it say?"

Sophie put down her phone. "People are unbelievable. There are already more than fifty comments threatening Jackson and Bubba. Some of them are really specific, like the things people want to do to them."

"I wonder if the people attacking Jackson and Bubba online will get investigated like Bubba's after his post." Esther's stomach flipped again.

"Right? I am no fan of Bubba and I'm angry, but not this mean."

Esther rubbed her eyes. "I can't look anymore. It's making me sick. Tell me if you see anything in the pictures or comments that helps. Maybe someone saw something."

"If I were Jackson or Bubba, I would be scared right now. We'd better talk to them tomorrow. If Kohornen decides they are suspects, he'll pick them up and they'll stop talking altogether. You said you know where they live, right?"

"I know where Bubba lives. We've seen him leave the trailer park and walk over to the school. Or I have, anyway."

"Do you know which trailer he lives in?" Sophie asked.

"No, but the park can't be that big. I'm sure we can ask someone. I've seen Jackson wait for the bus at the trailer park stop and, when his dad had his old truck, he parked it by the manager's office on the highway. So they must both live there."

"What if they did do it?" Sophie said. "It could be dangerous to go to the park and ask questions."

"You don't have to go. But I do. I'm terrified. But I'm more afraid of losing Parker without doing everything I possibly can. You know?" It was quiet. Esther looked over at Sophie and realized she had dropped her phone and fallen asleep.

Chapter Ten

The Costumes We Wear

Esther's mind never stopped spinning. She finally made notes about everything that happened at the dance. At the top of her list was to investigate Jackson and Bubba, then find out what Mr. Green threatened Aiden with and how he got his truck back. Then, as much as she liked Nevaeh, find out what happened to her father in the fire and her stepfather in the plane. *Maybe if we unravel the murder, we'll find what's making Parker so sick.*

Over and over she reviewed the night, trying to think of anything that would help. She gave up on sleep when the sun rose.

Miss Molly stretched lazily while she shook Sophie gently. "Soph. It's time to wake up and go to the hospital."

Sophie stretched just like Miss Molly, sat up, and rubbed the sleep out of her eyes. She took her round glasses off the desk and put them on.

Esther showered while Sophie brushed her teeth.

"Do nk they wl let . . ."

"What?" Esther spoke loudly over the sound of the shower.

Sophie rinsed her mouth and turned off the sink. "Do you think they will let us in to see him?"

"I hope so. Why wouldn't they?"

"I texted Nephi. He'll meet us in the kitchen and drive us up."

"Perfect." Esther rinsed the conditioner from her hair and quickly combed it.

Nephi parked near the main entrance to the rural hospital. Nestled in the trees, the hospital was about the same size as their small high school.

Esther checked her face again in the mirror on the passenger's visor. "I look tired, but I don't care."

"I don't feel like I slept at all." Sophie got out of the truck first.

"You slept. Trust me," Esther said.

"You both look great." Nephi used his key to lock the old manual locks and walked away from Sophie who stood with her mouth open in shock.

Nephi's tall body and long strides were hard to keep up with. They followed him through the double doors to the lobby. An older woman sat at the reception desk. Esther recognized her as Mrs. Murphy, Darlene's mom.

"Can I help ya'll?" She had a syrupy southern accent.

Sophie spoke up first. "We are here to visit Parker Stuart."

"I don't . . ." She peered at her computer screen and then picked up a clipboard and flipped through a few pages. "Oh. Hold on." She dialed a number and spoke into her headset. "Vern. Do you have Parker Stuart in the ward? ICU. I see. Oh. I see. Well, someone should have told me. I see. Uh-huh."

Esther was confused. She elbowed Sophie, who shook her head.

Mrs. Murphy hung up the phone. "Are you family?"

Esther shook her head, no.

"No one here by that name," Mrs. Murphy said.

"But . . ." Sophie started to say. She was interrupted by Mrs. Murphy, who repeated herself.

"No one here by that name."

Text to Paisley from Esther: *We are at Necanicum Hospital. Are you still here?*

Text from Paisley to Esther: *Yes! Coming right out.*

Sophie leaned on the receptionist's counter. "Listen, lady. We know our friend is here and you have to tell us what ward he is in and what room."

"Stand down, Sophie." Esther showed Sophie Paisley's reply on her phone screen. Then she showed Nephi, who straightened his hair.

"We'll just wait over here." Sophie pointed at a bronze statue of a whale breaching.

In less than a minute, Paisley flew through double doors and collided with Nephi in a desperate hug. "I missed you. This has been awful." At some point, she must have gone home and changed into jeans and a t-shirt. She was pale and had dark circles under her eyes.

Nephi held her. "I missed you too. How's he doing?" She stepped back, looking up into his face and then at Esther and Sophie.

"He is still out of it. They had to intubate him. You know? They put a tube down his throat to breathe for him. He stopped breathing last night. But now he seems stable to me. They ran a bunch of tests and the police were here asking my parents questions."

"What kinds of questions?" Concerned, Esther put her hands on her heart as if she could slow it down.

"That detective was asking if he experimented with drugs or ever had and how he knew Aiden Van Doren. He's dead. Did you hear?" Water gathered in her eyes, and she folded her arms. Nephi drew her into a hug. "What if Parker . . ."

"He won't." Esther sounded more certain than she felt.

"Can we go in and see him?" Sophie asked.

"No. Dad brought Mom and me some clothes. He's never alone. But the hospital won't let anyone beyond immediate family in. We weren't allowed to see him for hours while they worked on him. He's only been stable since a little before sunrise when they moved him from the emergency room to a larger room in the ICU."

"We should have brought flowers." Esther dug in her pockets for change. "Maybe something from the gift shop."

"You don't need to do that. Besides, I don't know if they let things like that into the rooms back there. He'll just be happy to see you when he wakes up."

"I hope that happens soon." Esther gave Paisley a small hug.

Nephi put his arm around Paisley. "I'm going to stay here."

"But you can't come back to the room." Paisley reached up and put her hand on his serious face. He kissed her fingers and held her hand.

"It's okay. I'll be here in the lobby if you need me. Can I bring your family some food?" Nephi asked.

Esther had never seen Nephi like this. His mouth was set in a firm line and he seemed serious, resolute. "Don't worry about us Nephi. We can walk home," Esther said.

Sophie poked her in the ribs with her elbow.

Esther glanced sideways at Sophie with raised eyebrows and said, "Right, Sophie?"

"Right."

"Thank you. You are the best friends a girl could have." Paisley hugged them both. "I'll text you if there is any change. I promise."

Esther and Sophie walked out into the crisp autumn morning. The trees clung to the last of their leaves. A cold gust of wind blew inland from the ocean.

Sophie zipped up her coat. "He's going to be fine. We're not really going home, right?"

"I hope he is. No. I want to try Jackson first. He seems more reasonable than Bubba."

They walked in silence for a moment. The only sound was the leaves crunching under their feet, as they walked down the hill along the long driveway surrounded by pine trees. A siren wailed in the distance, getting louder as it got closer. When they reached the main road, they watched the ambulance speed by, turn the corner, and race up the hill.

When the noise of the siren faded, Esther said, "Let's start by talking to Jackson. Let's see if he's at the tow shop. I think he works with his dad sometimes." Esther turned north on the road, and Sophie followed.

Sophie pulled up her hood to guard against the brisk wind. "Sounds like a plan. But let's not go in if his dad is there. It will be safer. You saw his dad threaten Van Doren."

"You don't have to go if you don't want to, Sophie. I wouldn't blame you."

Sophie kept walking by her side.

A little more than a mile down the road, a large, expensive looking church sat next to a row of dilapidated industrial shops, the tow shop being among them. Most of the paint was worn off the wood siding and the rest of the building was an industrial-sized garage door without windows. The Green Towing Company shop sign was painted and looked clean. Esther looked closely at a new sign above the door. "Do you think Jackson's dad painted his own sign?"

"It looks like it."

"It's brilliant. I wonder if he painted the logo on the side of his brand-new tow truck. I would be afraid to paint a car."

"The tow truck could be parked in the garage. I wish we knew where his dad is." Sophie peeked through the office window next to the door. "It looks like no one's here." She tried the door. It was locked.

"It's Sunday," Esther said. "Maybe they're closed and you're right, the truck is parked inside."

"I guess we try to find which trailers Jackson and Bubba live in. The trailer park is just on the other side of those trees. There's a trail to the park between those two buildings. When I rode the bus home from junior high, I saw kids who live there use the trail as a shortcut."

The gravel path snaked through the trees.

"This place is spooky," Esther said.

"We could call Papa J and ask him to go with us."

Esther squared her shoulders. "Remember how he responded to Bubba's post online? He wouldn't want us to talk to Jackson and Bubba. Do you have any better ideas?"

"Turn back time."

Esther smiled weakly. She and Sophie looked at each other. Side by side, they followed the trail. Logs and loose boards made a bridge over a small rivulet of water that probably became a stream during spring runoff. Ferns, vines, and berry bushes grew everywhere in the little woods. Even though they were less than two-tenths of a mile from Highway 101, all you could hear was the sound of birds and the wind blowing through the pine boughs. It smelled of loamy earth.

"If I wasn't so afraid, I would totally love this trail," Sophie said.

They stopped where the path split to get their bearings.

"There's a trailer right there." Sophie pointed at a small rise just beyond the next tree.

They quietly stepped closer. "It looks like the forest swallowed a trailer whole." All Esther could see was part of a cracked window peeking through ivy. Someone had put silver duct tape on the crack. Ferns and moss engulfed the back of the trailer, which was actually quite long, once she understood what she was seeing. There was only a partial cinderblock visible in the waist-high grass and ferns that grew under it. Moss and mold clung to the vinyl siding. Sophie got closer and wiped some moss away, exposing pink siding and the word *Ranchero* in chrome, or at least Esther guessed it was *Ranchero*. The cursive letters said *Rancher*. The letter *o* was missing.

"It's pretty big," Sophie said softly. "Let's go around front."

A deep bark began, and then the head of a massive pit bull appeared in the cracked window, slobbering on the dirty glass. The trailer rocked. Esther and Sophie jumped back. Sophie squealed and dug her nails into Esther's shaking arm.

"Can I help you?" Jackson Green said, rounding the corner. His long dark hair fell over one eye. Glaring at them through the other, he folded his arms and rose to his full height. "Down, Junkyard!" he said loudly over the dog. The dog whimpered, but they could still hear him pawing at the window.

Jackson was wearing the same red and navy-blue flannel shirt he'd worn to the dance.

Esther cleared her throat. "Actually, we're here because we're hoping you can help us,"

"Me? With what?" He raised his eyebrow and looked at them skeptically.

Esther's heart was pumping in her ears. A flash of her violent childhood interrupted her thoughts, but it was quickly replaced with Parker's face, writhing on the dance floor; the fear of losing him sharpened her focus.

"Did you know Adrian Van Doren died?" Esther asked.

Jackson's head snapped up, and he stepped back. He looked back and forth at their faces, and said, "What happened? He just looked sick. The ambulance took him. What killed him?"

Afraid, but more afraid of Parker dying, Esther said, "Parker is sick. Whatever killed Aiden made Parker so sick he isn't breathing on his own."

"For all we know, it could have been an accident," Sophie said. "The police think it might be something in the candy we all made. Someone could have spiked the punch. It's hard to tell."

"Are you blaming my dad?"

Esther studied his narrow, almost black eyes. An idea opened his eyes and he took a step closer, towering over her.

"You think me, and Bubba did it."

Esther stood her ground, trembling. "Right now, it doesn't matter who did it. All we care about is figuring out what made them sick, so the doctors know how to treat Parker. Maybe it was an accident, or a joke gone horribly wrong. Did you spike the punch or the food?"

He looked down and stood silently for a moment. "I didn't see anything."

"Did Bubba see anything? I know he was upset, but he seemed better at the dance," Sophie said.

Then his large eyes narrowed. "Look. I'd never harm a fly, and neither would Bubba. You've got him all wrong."

"Please, Jackson. I'm afraid Parker might die." Esther's voice shook ever so slightly.

His face softened for just a moment. Then he turned his back on them and started walking back around the trailer. Without thinking, Esther followed.

"Jackson. Please." She reached out and touched his arm gently. He froze. "Parker is sick. Don't you care?"

Jackson didn't turn around. "How's Paisley?"

Sophie rolled her eyes at Esther and shook her head. "How do you think? She's sitting with her twin, and he hasn't woken up since last night."

"I would never hurt anyone like that. Especially Parker or anyone in his family. Mr. Stuart has given me odd jobs, and Mr. Van Doren gave my dad a loan for a new tow truck. He has even invited Dad to workout at the gym with the other body builders. Not that dad would use the gym."

"Then help us, for Mr. Stuart's sake. What about Bubba?" Esther stepped toward him, desperation in her voice.

"I told you. You don't know him."

"Then tell us about him. Tell me what the secret was that Van Doren threatened your dad with." Esther said.

He searched Esther's eyes. "You don't know anything. You're wrong about Bubba."

Esther folded her arms and looked down her nose at him. "Then why did he post the picture. What makes you so sure he didn't do something?"

Jackson frowned, but after a moment his shoulders relaxed. "You better come in."

Esther and Sophie followed him on the narrow trail the rest of the way around the trailer. The forest opened into a clearing. Trailers, decaying picnic tables, and vehicles in various states of repair circled a cinderblock building that looked like it might contain bathrooms. But nothing was as they expected it to be.

Sophie's mouth fell open. Esther and Sophie froze for a moment, staring at the trailer park in front of them. "Oh my gosh! Who painted all of this?" Sophie waved her arm at the murals, and amazing artwork on the trailers and in the park.

He looked at his feet. His hair fell across his eyes again. He turned so she couldn't see his face.

"You created all this, didn't you? You drew Paisley, and you did this," Esther said. "It's amazing."

The bathroom was painted like a tiny witch's hovel with stones covering the cinderblock sides, vining flowers, and pieces of plywood painted on the roof to look like a thatched roof. It felt like they had crossed the ocean and were in a fairy tale.

Someone had buried large stones in the sandy soil in paths to the trailers and bathrooms. Esther turned to see Jackson, who was going into the trailer they had been behind. The front of the trailer looked nothing like the back. The trailer door had been painted to look like it was made of wood, like a castle door with ironwork and a stained-glass window. A trellis made from driftwood wrapped around the door and stuck out to create a covered walkway. It was covered with a flowering vine that took Esther's breath away.

She couldn't help herself. She touched one of the orange blossoms. "It's Clematis, you know, a vine?" Jackson said softly.

Around the base of the trailer were large round river rocks carefully piled and a deep blue cascade of flowers ran over the edges while dahlias stood tall everywhere.

He pointed at the flowers. "Blue heather. It shouldn't still be blooming, but it likes this protected corner. The weather's been mild, so the dahlias are still blooming. You can come in." Jackson walked toward the door and the girls followed.

When they got to the door, Esther couldn't help but reach out and touch the trailer's siding to see if the stone walls were real. They weren't, but they were so detailed it amazed her. She expected it to feel different.

"I had no idea you were a Madison Merriweather fan," Sophie said. "This is the house Fial lives in when he wishes he was at school in her first book."

Jackson's face turned red, but he smiled, and Esther realized his suspicious eyes had softened. It was like a small light turned on inside. He actually had a nice face when he wasn't mad.

Jackson's dog hit the other side of the door in another barrage of barking and scratching. Esther and Sophie jumped and grabbed each other.

"Junkyard! Down boy! Wait here." He cracked the door open and reached around it, taking the spiked collar of a snarling dog. Esther stepped back, her heart beating wildly, ready to retreat.

"That thing is a loaded weapon!" Sophie said.

Jackson shrugged, back to suspicious eyes, and went inside, closing the door. Esther heard movement and then he was back and opened the door. "Sorry. I put him in Dad's room. He can't get out."

The trailer was larger than Esther expected. Dust motes floated in the few shafts of light that made it through the broken window. Jackson flipped a switch by the door. Bright lights revealed unexpected magic. She had walked into one of Madison's books.

Although the house smelled like a dog, it looked clean. A wood-burning stove was on one end of the living room, with a dog's bed next to it. Two leather chairs faced a large, expensive television and gaming set.

It was the floor that fascinated her. Once again, Jackson had painted what she suspected was sheets of plywood to look like the stones of a castle floor. The walls were castle walls. Over the television, he had painted a family crest. The background was green, like his last name. A wizard and a dog were painted in the center.

"Brilliant!" Sophie walked over to examine the intricate artwork on the family crest.

There was a door that led outside directly opposite the front door. Esther hadn't noticed it when they were examining the back of the trailer. On the inside, he had painted it to look like it was open. Esther stepped in front of it. When you stood back, it felt like you could walk through the door to an English countryside and stroll down a long path to a castle on a hill in the distance.

"Bideford Castle College," Sophie informed Esther, who didn't want to admit she hadn't had time to read the new book and had only scanned the first book. "It feels like we've walked right into the story. I love it!"

Jackson's hands were buried deep in his pockets, and he was looking at his feet. If he heard Sophie, he didn't acknowledge it.

Esther spotted an easel in the corner. Beside it was a small table covered in paint tubes. There was a mason jar with brushes, rags, and a cutting board he was using as a pallet. On the easel was another piece of wood. It was an odd shape. She walked toward it.

"Don't . . ." Jackson reached out to stop her, but he was too late.

The painting took her breath away. It was of the sea and the cove in town. Winter storm clouds were rolling inland over a violent ocean. Waves crashed on the rocks, where she could see the side view of a girl that looked like Paisley Stuart. The figure had her blonde hair, in Paisley's favorite ponytail, her pert nose, angular face, and her long, lean frame in a long mint green dress, Paisley's favorite color. In the painting, Paisley stood alone on a large log, in danger of being swept out to sea. It was beautiful. She put her hand over her mouth and felt warmth spread from her chest to her toes.

Then she saw a stack of paintings. They were done on pieces of wood. Most of them faced the wall. She reached out to pick one up, drawn in by his surprising and inspiring talent.

"No." He stepped between her and his artwork. "They're stupid."

"No, they're not. They're amazing. Let me look. Please?"

He studied her face and bit his lower lip. "Don't tell anyone. Promise?"

"On my mother's grave." Esther looked at Sophie, who nodded. Her mother didn't have a grave.

One by one, she and Sophie turned the paintings around. They were seascapes, local lighthouses, the jetty, the harbor. There was a common theme. A beautiful muse. Paisley appeared in almost half. Then to her surprise, she recognized herself in the robes from the movie in the summer. She looked like a wild witch standing on top of a sand dune with a sailing ship on the ocean.

She looked at him, but he only looked down, embarrassed. "I don't remember this in the book."

"I saw the party," he chuckled softly. "The cast party when they passed out the robes? It was my pirate phase. Every painting had to have a ship or a pirate in it."

"I'm surprised you didn't put a sail on your house." Sophie grinned at Jackson and he openly smiled back.

"That's a great idea." They laughed together.

"Jackson," Esther said. "I don't understand. Why do you hide this? Why don't you let the kids at school know how gifted you are?"

"I am just a poor kid from the Mossy Rock trailer park."

"Your dad owns the best tow truck in town. And what's wrong with being poor? I'm not rich." Esther gently stacked his paintings back where they were?"

Jackson let out a sarcastic belly laugh. "Not rich? Are you kidding me? I've seen your house. Okay, so Dad has a truck. But you saw how close we are to losing it."

"Hey. How did you get it back?" Sophie asked.

Jackson was quiet for a moment. He studied their faces.

He reminds me of me. He doesn't know who he can trust.

"That's my dad's business."

"You can trust us. We aren't going to tell anyone. We promise." Sophie held up her well-used pinky, "Pinky promise."

He shook his head at her ridiculous gesture.

Esther said softly, "Jackson, someone is dead. Is there anything you know or saw that will help us find out what happened to Aiden and Parker? We need to know so the doctors can fix it."

"Well, it wasn't me. I may be poor, but that doesn't mean I'm a violent criminal. Sure, I was mad about Nephi getting us in trouble at school and having to decorate and help with the dance when I couldn't even afford to buy a ticket."

Esther repeated the question, "Then how could you afford to get your dad's truck back?"

He sighed. "I haven't asked him. Aiden returned the truck to my dad. They were still yelling at each other when someone from the car lot picked Aiden up. Dad hated him because of the truck, and I don't see that changing even after he's dead."

She nodded. "Jackson?" Esther had another thought. "I see your dad towing people all the time. Where does his money go?" Esther realized Jackson was thin. Sure, they had a big-screen television, but did they have food? The small kitchen was through an open doorway painted like a castle archway. She walked over to the fridge.

"Don't!"

She ignored him and opened the door. There was a gallon of milk. A small brick of cheese, a loaf of bread, condiments, and jam—prescription bottles, a lot of them. Jackson pushed the refrigerator door closed and leaned back on it.

"That isn't a lot of food," Esther said.

"I eat at school when I'm not suspended. That's why I was so mad at Nephi."

Esther's heart ached. She shook her head and left the clean and tidy kitchen. "Jackson, you don't have to live like this."

"I'm not going back to foster care." His words were firm and said through clenched teeth.

"Why? The Ironpots are foster parents. Mrs. Ironpot is an awesome cook." Sophie cocked her head and looked confused. "Who wouldn't want to live with them?"

"Me. Bubba. I need my paints and space to create. And I'd miss Junkyard."

"And your freedom?" Esther asked. Jackson nodded. "So, you were in foster care and the Ironpots were your foster parents. Why did you have to go into care?"

He let out a long sigh, deflated. "I guess you might as well know it all. You have enough on me now to totally humiliate me in front of the whole school."

"Spill." Sophie stood resolute and Esther waited, hoping he would tell the truth.

"Dad has a gambling problem. I make him give me money each day for the rent or food as soon as he earns it. Sometimes I use it to buy paint or brushes, but I get the wood free from the carpenter's scrap heap by Dad's shop. I was also supposed to make the payment on the truck, but dad didn't bring home enough money."

"But your dad is always towing someone, and that doesn't explain foster care." Esther knew she was pushing him, but Parker's life was on the line.

"Dad and Bubba's dad went to jail. They weren't there long, but child protective services got involved. Mrs. Ironpot still likes to stop by and check on me sometimes. They're real nice."

"Why did your dad go to jail?" Sophie asked.

"He got into a fight at the bar over video poker with this tourist. I don't know the details, but the tourist was a big guy and somehow, the tourist died during the fight. Bubba's dad and my dad were friends from before I was born. His dad was working at the bar and got into the middle of the fight. They were arrested for manslaughter and possession. Dad was on probation for a long time. Bubba's dad died after they got out of prison."

"Wait. Bubba's dad is dead?" Esther was surprised. She knew he lived with his mom, but not that his dad was dead. "How did he die? When did this happen?"

"Overdose. The day he got out of jail. He didn't calculate right after being sober for the year they were in jail. It was a while ago. Anyway, you should talk to Bubba about that. Seriously. You are going to get me in so much trouble with him if you tell him you know. He's my best friend. He gets embarrassed, you know?"

"Why?" Sophie's brows knit together in confusion.

"Because privileged, wealthy brats like you wouldn't understand our lives."

"He doesn't know me." Sophie folded her arms.

"Only someone with your privilege would say that. You don't know him. What if he needs a job? Would you hire him after you heard he threatened students at the high school? What about his little brothers and sisters? Who is going to explain it to them when kids at school bully them because he's their brother? It stinks out there."

"Where?" Sophie tilted her head, curious.

"The world. The whole world stinks."

"You better hope not", Sophie said. "Because once that world sees your artwork, they are going to want to give you money for it, and then you're going to be wealthy."

"I don't need money."

"You shouldn't hide your gift. Let us help you. Hey. Where's your mom?" Esther hadn't seen any sign of a woman in the trailer or yard.

He just shrugged. It was a non-answer. Because Esther hated questions about her father, she let it go. She knew the look on his face. But she also knew it was time to get to the other reason they were there.

"Okay," Esther said. "Do you know what secret your dad was holding over Aiden's head?"

Jackson didn't answer. He looked down at the floor without saying a word.

"Do you know who might have put something in the food that killed Mr. Van Doren?"

"How do you know it was the food? How do you know they aren't just like Bubba's dad, and they OD'd?" He talked about death like it was just a fact of life.

"What makes you think it might be drugs?" Esther asked.

"Rich dude like that. Pretty boy. Money to burn. Maybe they got bored and tried something new for the dance, and it was out of their league? Have you ever thought of that?"

"Parker would never . . ."

He interrupted her. "You don't know what people will do. You live . . ."

Esther cut him off. "Okay. So, my house is nice. But I am well aware of what people can do and say. You aren't the only one who's had a rough life. But you have talent that could change your life. Don't be like me. Don't hide from the bad things because you'll miss out on the good things." She surprised herself. *Where did that lecture come from?*

"What's wrong with hiding? I hate it out there. I just gotta get through school and then out of this dump."

"Dump?" Sophie sounded shocked. "This is the most beautiful place I have ever seen. I would love to live here. I love everything in Madison's books. She would love this."

"Oh, right. The lady with the real castle."

"You don't know her. She's nice. She would totally love this." Esther stood up for Sophie. She knew she was right. *We're getting nowhere. Parker needs us to figure this out.*

Esther tried to think in the pressured silence. She finally just asked the first question that popped into her head. "Is it possible that Bubba spiked the punch or did something?"

"You don't understand." Jackson took his cell phone out of his back pants pocket and started texting.

Sophie looked at Esther and rolled her eyes. "Can you help us understand?"

Jackson took a coat off a hook by the door and put it on. "Follow me." He left them standing in his living room. The front door swung shut. Both girls looked at each other and shrugged. They pushed the door open and saw that long-legged Jackson was already halfway across the trailer park.

A cold breeze shook the pines. Esther zipped her hoodie up, and they jogged to catch up with Jackson. The grass between stone paths and along the gravel circular drive was brown and crunchy under her feet. She could see Sophie's breath make clouds in the crisp air.

Trailers in the park were in various states of disrepair. An ancient white trailer with blue trim had three broken windows with plastic over them. one trailer had a large extension cord running out of one and into a little trailer's window. A woman in a large purple coat sat on the steps of the small trailer smoking and examining them.

Jackson passed the blue and white trailer and took the next gravel road. It wound into the woods with random trailers, campers, and even a tent hidden in tall pine trees. The air smelled of pine, soil, and cigarettes. For a tenth of a mile, they walked through the silent forest with no sign of any other trailer until they came to a clearing.

From the edge of the clearing, they could see it was littered with tricycles, wagons, bicycles, and homemade plywood jumps. Kids were everywhere, laughing, riding, and playing. A car with only three wheels was balanced on wooden blocks. Under the cover of a make-shift roof was a long brown trailer with a patchwork add-on.

Baxter Jones sat in the car on blocks. "Finn! Finn! Knock it off. Give her back the wagon." He got out of the car and strode across the patchy lawn to a rusty Radio Flyer wagon. Two children in overalls were fighting over it. Esther guessed they were about four years old. They both had dirty faces, but one had short hair, while the other had long, curly blonde hair. They were exactly the same height. A small black dog sat next to the wagon watching, but not moving.

"Bubba," Jackson called.

Bubba turned to look straight at them. His brows drew together, and he frowned, glaring at the girls with his pale, gray-blue eyes. His grungy, blond hair hung in hanks. "What."

They crossed the clearing to meet him. He folded his arms and looked down, towering over a foot and a half above Sophie's short frame, and a foot over Esther. He smelled like grease, oil, and sweat.

"Why did you bring them here?"

"Did you hear? Mr. Van Doren died and Parker's in the hospital." Jackson scanned the yard. "And Frankie is in your car, dude." A skinny boy in a dirty white t-shirt that had a picture of Sasquatch on the front was pretending to steer the derelict car.

"Frankie! Get out of there."

Frankie took one look at Bubba, who was running toward him, and he scampered out the window on the other side of the car. Laughing, he ran for all he was worth into the woods. The small black dog barked and chased him. Bubba looked at the steering wheel and pulled a screwdriver out of the ignition.

He put it in his pocket and came back to Esther and Sophie. "Why is Parker in the hospital?"

"We don't know, but we suspect whatever killed Van Doren is the same thing that made Parker sick," Sophie said. "Who are all the kids? Are you running a daycare? Are these kids for sale?"

Bubba threw his head back and laughed, hard. "I'll sell them. What'll you give me for Frankie? Wait—I'll pay you to take Frankie."

"Bubba!" Frankie came out from behind a fallen pine tree and glared at Bubba. "I'm telling Mom."

"Go for it!" Bubba laughed even harder. Jackson laughed with him. When their laughter died down, Bubba said, "In fact, I'll pay you to take them all."

"But not me, Bubba. Not me." A tiny girl in a pink dress that looked like Bubba with long braids tugged at his shirt.

He scooped her up and threw her in the air. "No, Gladys. Never Gladys. Glad to meet ya, Gladys." She giggled and hugged his neck. He sat her down, and she ran to Frankie.

"Who did her hair?" Esther asked.

Jackson chuckled. "Bubba."

Bubba punched Jackson hard in the shoulder, making Jackson laugh harder. A baby started to cry.

"Now look what you did." Bubba shook his head, disgusted. He marched inside the trailer door and came back out with a complaining bundle wrapped in a green blanket.

"Oh!" Sophie lit up like a Christmas tree. "A baby."

"No, a puppy," Bubba said sarcastically.

"Can I hold him?" Sophie reached out. Esther had never seen her like this. But she had also never seen her around a baby before.

"I guess." Bubba looked down at Sophie with one eyebrow raised. "Ready?"

"I've never held a baby before." She reached for the bundle and took it from Bubba. Putting it on her shoulder, she patted the baby on the back. "Will he burp?"

"She. Fern. And you've really never held a baby before?" Brows raised, Bubba chuckled.

"I think this one is leaking."

"Fern." Bubba took her back inside.

"Who are all the kids?" Esther asked Jackson.

"Bubba's brothers and sisters."

"How many does he have?"

"Did you see the tattoo on his wrist? The ten? He's one of ten."

"Is he the oldest?" Esther counted. She saw seven kids of various ages and sizes playing in the yard. A van driven by a middle-aged woman pulled down the road. A tall girl who looked a little younger than Bubba got out and eyed them suspiciously before she went into the trailer. The van left and Bubba came out without the baby.

"Francine is home. Let's go down to the creek. She'll watch everyone for a bit. But I can't go far."

They followed him around the trailer and down a short trail. The woods opened onto a rocky beach. A shallow creek ran through the clearing. There was a ring of stones and the remains of a fire on the beach. Someone had put four logs around it. He sat on one. Jackson sat across from him, and the girls sat on the log facing the creek.

"This is beautiful," Esther said. It was cold. She pushed her hands deep into her hoodie pockets and watched crystal clear water run around rocks.

"We don't let the kids come here without Mom or me. They can't swim and the creek can get deep enough to drown someone."

"Where is your mom?" Esther asked.

"She's a nurse. She usually works three twelves on swing shift over the weekends. She's asleep."

Esther nodded. Deep in thought. *Nothing about Bubba or Jackson is what I thought it was. But does that mean they aren't killers? What if they're just good liars? What if Bubba did it and Jackson hasn't got a clue? A prank gone wrong? And what were the pills in the refrigerator of all places?*

"Look, Bubba," Esther wrung her hands and plead with him. "I know you've been mad at us. But all I care about right now is saving Parker. I am terrified he'll die. You don't want that, do you? If you know what was in the food or punch or how they got sick—please, please tell us. And if you did it because you were mad, it's okay. Just tell us what you put in the food."

A cloud of anger rolled across Bubba's face. He jumped up to his entire six-foot six-inch height. He felt like her father, thunder, ferocity, and a size that made her feel small enough to crush. Esther stayed seated. It took everything she had not to run. *I am not a child. He is not my father. Stay in the present, Esther . . .* She felt someone touch her arm. Sophie looked at her through her round black glasses. The touch was enough to stop her headlong decent into the past.

"I would never do something like that to anyone," Bubba said slowly and deliberately.

"Then why did you post the picture of the school on fire?" Sophie stood up and took a step in his direction.

He deflated like a day-old balloon and sat back down. "I was mad. I meant like, you know, burn in heck. My mother grounded me for a month. I didn't even think she would let me go to the ball. Now I wish I hadn't."

"So, you don't want to burn the school down with us in it?" Esther asked.

Jackson chuckled and shook his head. Bubba rubbed his face with his hands.

"I didn't really think it through when I made the post."

"Maybe you did something the night of the ball you didn't think through?" Esther said.

His head snapped around, frowning, anger rising quickly and unpredictably, like a bolt of unexpected lightening. He spoke through gritted teeth. "I just got so mad when Nephi kicked Jackson in the stomach. Jackson's my best friend. He's more like a brother. I don't care if Nephi's your brother, he's an arrogant rich boy."

"We're not rich! I don't know where you got that idea. Nephi's my uncle, and we have to share the same house because we're not rich. My mother was a single mom too. Nephi's mom, my grandma, only has us. You don't know anything about us." She leaned toward him, provoking him, ignoring her shaking hands. *He's explosive.*

"Yeah? Well, I saw that house when I ran long distance track. Nephi has his own truck. I don't know what you think rich is, but in my world, you are. You have your own house, it's huge and in a nice neighborhood. You have three or four cars, and they all run. Everyone had new shoes for track. That's what I call rich." Bubba sneered at Esther and chuckled.

"Is that a threat? You know where I live?" Esther said.

He folded his arms, frowning. The silence was tangible as he glared at her.

He's right. I am rich. Okay, I don't have a lot of money, but in his world, I have a ton compared to his family. But he's also unpredictable. He could have done something in a fit of rage without thinking about the lethal consequences.

"Did anyone else ask you to put something in the food or punch?" Esther asked.

Bubba rolled his eyes. "No."

"Did you see or experience anything unusual the night of the dance?" Esther asked.

"You mean besides puking up punch and apples in the parking lot?" Bubba laughed. "Everything was weird. That's the first time I'd gone to one of those. The tickets weren't cheap. Ms. Priest got us some for helping. A bunch of mean, rich kids if you ask me. Principal Kelly was talking to Jackson's dad in the parking lot, but that's not weird, is it Jackson?" he chuckled. "He was either asking his dad for a little something to get through the dance or telling him to move along."

"Wait. Back up. You threw up?" Sophie asked. "Did you have any other symptoms?"

"I didn't sleep for two days. I am allergic to apple peel, but the rock candy apple looked cool. I wanted to try it. I ate chocolate, drank punch, ate candy, and loved it. I should have known better than to eat an apple. That's probably why I threw up."

"What usually happens when you eat them?" Esther asked.

"My tongue and my throat itch. Sometimes my lips swell. I don't know why I even took a bite of one."

"But you've been fine ever since?" Sophie squinted and tilted her head. "No other side effects?"

"He hasn't been okay since the day he was born." Jackson laughed at his own joke. Bubba looked up and grinned.

Jackson has a nice smile, but his eyes are like two black holes—hard to read.

The sound of a baby crying blew in with the wind. "I need to get back. Francine doesn't know how to keep Fern happy." He started to walk away and then he turned around and said, "I really hope Parker gets better, and I am sorry Mr. Van Doren passed away." He trotted away and disappeared through the trees.

"Are you done jumping to conclusions?" Jackson sat down opposite the girls.

"Honestly? Anyone could have spiked the punch or put something in the food. All I know is we still don't know why Parker is sick or what killed Mr. Van Doren. I don't know why Principal Kelly and Aiden Van Doren wanted to see your dad, but if it had to do with pills like the ones in your fridge, then just tell us so we can let the hospital know what it is." Esther looked at Sophie who nodded. "I would be thrilled with an anonymous call to the police so Parker can be treated. I bet a judge would be more lenient too."

"Those pills were prescribed. For all you know it was Nevaeh," Jackson said.

"What?" Sophie leaned forward.

He looked Esther in the eyes. "How do you know it wasn't Nevaeh? Huh? Why do you always assume it's the kids from the wrong side of the tracks, like me? Maybe she's one of those girls that smiles at you while they plan a way to kill you at the prom."

"Kohornen suspects you. You left early, and you threatened kids at school on social media. No matter who did it; we need to know what they used, or we can't help Parker. Blaming you is the easy answer. You could be Kohornen's only suspects. Help us, Jackson, and you'll help yourself." Esther started to get up.

"Your art is amazing. I really hope you didn't do it," Sophie said.

Jackson got up slowly. Esther watched his tired movements. There was a sadness in his sloped shoulders and his eyes always hidden in his hair.

"Jackson?" Esther was surprised to hear the sound of her own voice. But what she wanted to say was burning in her chest and had to come out. He stopped walking but didn't look at her. "I may have misjudged you."

His head snapped up and one brown eye looked at her, narrow, confused.

"Not just because we need your help to find out what happened to Parker, but because we were wrong about a lot of things about you."

She felt a sharp kick in her shin by a tiny pointy foot. "What she means to say is as long as you lay off of Paisley, and you aren't fighting with Nephi, you're not half bad." Sophie squinted at him, hands on her hips.

A slow smile spread across Jackson's face. It was like a light coming on in the dark. "Got it." He stood up taller, breathed deeply, and kept smiling as they walked the trail back to Bubba's trailer.

Esther heard the sound of the baby screaming coming from the direction of Bubba's house. Then the sound of kids yelling Bubba's name. Then a familiar voice. "Hey, kid! Stop kicking me. He's fine." Her heart leapt into her throat. She started to run with Sophie and Jackson following her on the narrow trail.

They rounded the corner and ran into complete chaos. Papa J was in uniform by his squad car. Bubba was in the backseat yelling. Francine was holding Fern and screaming at Hart, while the baby wailed in her arms, flailing, red in the face. "You've got no right! Let him out! Bubba! Open that door!"

Finn and his twin were pounding on Hart's legs. Gladys, the round-faced tiny girl, was standing by Francis crying so hard tears poured down her bright red face as she held her pudgy hands out toward the squad car. Gladys stomped in place and her diaper sagged. The dog was growling and pulling at Hart's pant leg. Hart was trying to get in his squad car, but he couldn't peel the kids off.

Frankie ran toward Hart with a raised baseball bat. Jackson moved quickly and grabbed the bat, stopping Frankie dead in his tracks. "Mom!" Frankie bellowed, but he was looking at Jackson.

Esther realized a tired-looking woman who looked younger than her mom and much, much thinner, was talking to Ironpot on the porch. She was crying and so were the two twin girls that looked just like Bubba clinging to her legs. Esther couldn't hear a word over all the chaos.

"Frankie! Frankie! Finn! Get inside. Fanny!" The thin woman called the kids into the trailer while she held the door open. Frankie glared at Esther but followed the last twin into the trailer.

Horrified, Esther said, "Papa J. Why are you arresting Bubba?"

He gave her a thin-lipped serious look and then turned his attention to Jackson. "Jackson, we need you to come down to the station to answer some questions."

"I need to call my dad."

"How old are you, son?"

"Eighteen. Almost nineteen. I got held back."

"Get in the car. You can call him from the station, or we can let him know where you are."

"Papa J?" Esther said. "Please . . ." A tear fell on her cheek and she angrily wiped it. She hated it when she cried in public. She wasn't sad. She was furious.

"Esther. I don't know what you're doing here, but this isn't the place for you. This trailer park . . ." He stopped short when Jackson's head snapped around and he balled his hands into fists. "Anyway. Go home. We'll talk at home."

Ironpot got in the passenger door of the squad car.

"Why don't you just work on being a friend to Parker and his family? They need it now more than ever." Hart got in the squad car and circled across the lawn, over the baseball bat, and drove back down the drive.

Shocked, Esther and Sophie watched the car leaving in a cloud of dust rising above the gravel road.

Chapter Eleven

Pumpkins & Mice

Sophie and Esther walked back toward the hospital on the hill. Sophie walked backwards in front of Esther, her arms waving as she explained her epiphany to Esther.

"Don't you see?"

"Sort of. So, you think Nevaeh loved Mr. Van Doren so much that if her mom couldn't have him, no one could. Like he took the place of her dead father, and she has a weird fixation?"

"Exactly," Sophie said. She turned around and walked alongside Esther. "And now we know, or I think we know, there was something wrong with the caramel apples, chocolate, or punch at the dance."

"Or, Bubba had an allergic reaction to the apples."

"But he said when he reacted to apples it made his throat itch, normally. Apples haven't made him throw up. We need to do some online research or ask when we get to the hospital. Or I need to see if I can get my parents to help me in their lab and look at the apple we have."

"Nevaeh was really upset during the meeting. And she has seen a lot of death in her lifetime. I really like her. I mean, I love how authentic she seems. But you always tell me how nice serial killer are."

"Sometimes kids do terrible things when they're under pressure," Sophie said.

"Like, what if she accidentally set the fire that killed her father? I don't know," Esther said.

A gust of cold wind tugged at Sophie's hair. "Historically, when the news interviews the neighbors of famous serial killers, they all say the same thing. 'He was such a nice guy.' Nevaeh is a blast, but people do make mistakes. I don't think we can count her out, yet. Even if we want to. She might have been trying to get back at Aiden for leaving her mom for Ms. Priest."

"For all we know it was some random kid playing a prank or Jackson's dad. There were so many people there," Esther said.

"I guess. What if it's Principal Kelly? Maybe his bad dad jokes are a cover? If he goes to jail, we won't have to listen to them anymore."

"Now we're reaching," Esther chuckled.

Sophie shrugged and blew on her hands to warm them up. "When is it going to get any warmer?" She pulled up the hood on her coat.

"Next August. Do you know what I feel bad about when I think about Bubba?" Esther stopped at the bottom of the hospital driveway. The wind blew through the bare branches of the maple trees that lined the drive. Gray clouds rolled south, pushed by a cold northeastern wind.

Sophie looked at her and waited patiently.

Esther sorted through her thoughts while the wind pushed her forward and blew autumn leaves across the road. "There for the grace of God, go I."

"What do you mean?" Sophie asked.

"If my mom and I hadn't had Grandma Mable and Nephi to chip in and come with us, my mom wouldn't have been able to afford the house. Did you know money from the sale of Grandma Mable's house helped buy our Necanicum house? Mom would have had to get child-care. She wouldn't be able to work on-call like she does or be able to leave in the middle of the night without leaving us alone. It's expensive to take someone to daycare, and Mary would have been kicked out of every single one. I could have been babysitting like Bubba."

"Mary needs a room in the monkey house at the zoo." Sophie grinned.

Esther chuckled. "Yeah. She is unique. But honestly, I could have been in the same trailer park, babysitting, and not doing well at school. I don't know how he gets any homework done in that chaos. And he's so thin. So is his mom. I could have been just like Bubba or Jackson if life had taken any other path. I never realized how much Grandma Mable and Mom have been able to do for us."

"Well, your mom is educated."

"So is Bubba's mom. She's a nurse. My mom didn't finish college. She's just trained. When we had to do a career search for a school assignment, Mom suggested I think about nursing because it pays well. Bubba's mom was just left with a larger family. See? If it weren't for the blessing of Grandma and a little luck, that could have been me."

"Not me."

"Right," Esther laughed. "God wouldn't give you nine brothers and sisters because you would kill one."

"Darn straight, I would. All that crying and leaking from everywhere. Oh, and the smell of that baby? Sour milk and . . ."

"Okay! Don't make me gag."

"She was so cute," Sophie smiled.

"Hey! I have an idea."

"Oh, no."

Esther never got to share her idea. Nephi was driving down the gravel road in their direction. He stopped and rolled down the window. "There's no point in going up there. He's worse."

Esther's heart dropped.

"I'm sorry, Esther."

She couldn't respond. She couldn't breathe.

Nephi reached out of the truck window and gave her shoulder an unusual squeeze. "I'm going to get some food and bring it back for their lunch. I'm just hoping they'll eat it."

"Do you need some money?" Sophie said.

"No. Paisley's father gave me a credit card and a list. I think he's worried about his wife and Paisley." He waved and pulled away.

"Do you want to go back to your house?" Sophie asked.

"I want to leave a note for Parker and stay nearby." Esther kept walking and Sophie followed. "I wish I had something to give him."

They passed through the automatic electric doors and stood quietly just inside. Mrs. Murphy, their friend Darlene's mom, was still at the front desk. She looked up and took off her glasses. "Oh, you sweet darlings," she drawled. "Such a state you're in. I am so sorry, darlin, about your boyfriend. He's tough, but anyone can fail when it comes to this."

"What do you mean? Is he . . ."?

"Oh, no!" She held her hands up and waved away her words. "I just mean drugs, darlin. They're so tempting. Who wouldn't fall into it?"

When Esther realized what she was saying, her anger flared. "Please don't gossip, Mrs. Murphy. You don't know what happened."

"Why darlin, I most certainly do. Your boyfriend has himself in a peck of trouble and you probably used the same stuff he did to land in this place."

Anger boiled in Esther. She didn't understand what Mrs. Murphy was trying to say. She was still trying to put the pieces together when Sophie stepped closer to Mrs. Murphy's desk.

Sophie leaned on the desk. "Well, you're going to get yourself in more than a peck of trouble. You're violating patient confidentiality and my parents are scientists, so I know. You just need to keep your mouth shut."

"Wait. Wait. What are you saying?" Esther said.

"I'm saying your boyfriend was doing something he shouldn't 'ought a do. It wasn't my friend Angelica Rose's food that poisoned that boy."

"Stop talking in riddles. What are you trying to tell us?" Sophie leaned further over the desk.

Mrs. Murphy leaned close to her. "I'm saying he was doing bad things. He's probably been hanging around that . . ."

"Esther." Esther turned to see her mother at the double doors. Her arms were folded over her black hoodie. And her brows were furrowed, matching the concerned look on her face.

"Uh, oh. Hi, Mom," Esther said cheerfully. She put a smile on her face and tried to trot lightly across the lobby to her mother.

"Esther and Sophie. Step outside please."

Esther felt her heart pick up the pace and the heat from her neck burned around to her face and warmed her cheeks. She was sure she was bright red. Her mother walked outside the automatic glass doors and the girls joined her. The glass doors sealed behind them.

Esther looked at Sophie who raised her eyebrows, shrugged, and mouthed the words, *why is she mad?* Esther shrugged in reply.

When they'd walked a few yards away from the door, her mother stepped into an alcove cut into the side of the building. It was filled with green vegetation with a statue of a whale in the center and two cement benches. But Esther's mother didn't sit down. Instead, she stood next to the whale, arms still folded.

"I got a call from Hart that he ran into you in a dangerous part of town."

"Dangerous? Kids from school live there," Esther said. She tried to use her most innocent tone.

"Esther. You know you're not supposed to be down there."

"I know . . . But Mom, you should have been there. And the people that live there are nice. And we're not kids anymore."

"You're still young, and kids your age disappear all the time. You didn't tell me where you were going. And trust me, not all the people who live there are good."

Sophie stood quietly, looking back and forth between Esther and her mother.

"I know we should have told you we were going there and I'm sorry. But it's not what you think." Esther searched for a way to explain what they experienced to her mother but couldn't find the words fast enough.

"I do know, Esther. Remember what I do for a living? I've been down there."

"But not to Jackson's trailer or Bubba's."

Her mother didn't answer. Esther studied her mother's face. Her mother was still a wall of anger. "You know I can't talk about my job. What I can talk about is you. I understand how frightened you must be about Parker. It's awful. But the thought of losing you is my worst nightmare. Bubba was just in trouble for threatening you."

Esther interrupted her mother. "But if I were a boy like Nephi, would you be lecturing me?" Esther raised her eyebrows and waited, smug in the knowledge that this was one of her mother's soft spots: fairness.

Esther's mother breathed out hard, and unfolded her arms, putting her hands in her jean's pockets. "I guess that's true. He is older and larger, and I should be fair. I will tell you what. If you feel the need to see Jackson or Bubba at home again, you will call me. Don't forget the online threat. We know Bubba did it."

"Thanks, Mom." Esther stepped forward to hug her mother.

Her mother put her hand out and stopped her. "But! You will let me know where you are going and when you'll be home and if at all possible, you will take Nephi with you. Now. How is Parker?"

And just like that, Esther knew the discussion was over, but Esther knew her mother would ground her when she got home. Her mother knew Esther would do what she was told in the future, but there would still be consequences. "He is on a ventilator and the receptionist was so mean."

Sophie jumped into the conversation. "She shared private medical information. She made it sound like Parker was on drugs and he chose to take them. Isn't that against the Hippy Rules?"

"H.I.P.A.A. Health Insurance Portability and Accountability Act. And violating it could cost Mrs. Murphy her job. Should we report her or are you glad to know what's going on?"

"Both?" Esther grinned.

Her mother smiled. "Sorry, honey. Life doesn't work that way. But she probably hasn't violated anything. It is on the newspaper website and in my email. The headlines read *Man Dies of Narcotic Overdose*. But it didn't list the drug. Did she tell you?" One of her mother's brows raised. She stared at Esther while the question hung in the air.

"Not yet. We didn't know they had discovered what killed Aiden."

"Leave whatever you wanted to leave for Parker and then let me take you two home." Her mother smiled affectionately.

"We didn't have anything to leave. I'm so worried, Mom."

"Let's take a quick trip to the gift shop. I'll buy a mylar balloon and a card for Parker. We can all sign the card."

They were walking to her mother's Jeep when Mr. Green's tow truck roared into the parking lot and pulled in front of them, cutting them off. The tinted electric window rolled down and Mr. Green leaned out. "My boy's with the police and I hear you two was at my place. I don't know what happened, but you stay away from my boy!"

Esther realized her mother had both her arms out, spread across their chests, protecting them.

Suddenly, her mom pushed them back and took one step forward. She said forcefully, "If you have a beef, it is with me, Mr. Green. Clean your own glass house before you start throwing stones."

He rolled up his window and roared out of the parking lot.

"Whoa, Mrs. Hart. You're like Xena, warrior princess!" Sophie did the victory sign.

Then her mom whirled around on them. "And you two. Trust me. Stay away! Now. It's Sunday, and I've come to the conclusion that you both need more time in church."

Wide-eyed, Esther and Sophie looked at each other, and then quietly followed her to the car.

Chapter Twelve

Paying the Price of the Ticket

Sunday dinner at Esther's house was a lazy affair. Church was over and the whole family moved like they were swimming in molasses. Nephi eventually came back and fell asleep on the couch watching a movie with Esther's mom and Grandma Mable. Mary had every Barbie in her collection out, including their horses and pets. Her thriving Barbie farm was set up in front of the fireplace. The fire crackled and warmed the room while the wind occasionally pushed at the old windows and doors, whistling on the way in.

Esther had an unread book in her lap and rocked in the chair by the fire, texting back and forth between Sophie, Nephi, and Paisley. Even Nevaeh and Bridget were talking in a group text. Everyone wanted to know how Parker was doing. Paisley said there still was no news. She hadn't passed on the gossip from Mrs. Murphy. She knew Parker would never use drugs or break the rules and drink. Not knowingly, at least. Kids at Oceanside High had been known to spike the punch before, but this—this was different. This drug had killed a man, or he'd overdosed.

Nevaeh said she felt better. She had thrown up after the party like Bubba. She said she didn't remember much until she woke up late Sunday morning. If she wasn't affected by the drug, it was the worst virus she'd ever had.

Text to Nevaeh: *Are you going to tell the police?*

Text from Nevaeh: *Mom's seriously upset about the accusation from some people that there was something wrong with the food. She said it could affect the business. I don't want to make it worse. I'm not bringing it up.*

Text to Nevaeh: *Accidents happen. Could it have been an accident?*

Text to Esther: *No. You saw how clean our candy room is. Everyone can see it through the glass behind the counter in the store.*

Text to Nevaeh: *Did anyone else have access to the food before the party?*

Text to Esther: *Just the employees. I guess anyone could have gotten into it if they wanted to bad enough. But why? To hurt Mom?*

Text to Nevaeh: *Does someone want to hurt her?*

Nevaeh didn't answer. Esther waited for the little bubble that indicated she was typing. Nothing.

Text to Paisley: *How is he? How are you?*

Between gusts of wind, Esther heard Papa J's Jeep Cherokee pull into the driveway. Usually, he jogged happily up the stairs, but the footsteps this evening were different. Slow, methodical steps halted on the other side of the door. She noticed her mother, Nephi, and Grandma were all looking at the quiet door, waiting for it to open.

Mary bolted and yanked the door open. "Papa J! She threw herself around his legs. He caught her and then grabbed the door jamb, so she didn't knock him over.

"Hi, baby girl." He leaned over and let her hug his neck while he picked her light frame up and carried her back inside.

Esther could see the trees whipping in the wind behind him. The automatic porch light came on late, just as he was closing the door. Mary slid down to the floor and yanked on his arm. "Come see my farm."

"Honey, let him have a minute. Why don't you go get your pj's on?" Esther's mom stood up and hugged Papa J. Mary shot past her and took the stairs for her room with a naked Barbie in each hand.

This was the first time that Esther had seen Papa J since he arrested Jackson and Bubba. She didn't want to make eye contact. Her stomach rolled and she wished she had skipped eating popcorn. Part of her was angry they'd taken the boys in like that, but her common sense reminded her that it was his job.

"Esther." He was looking at her. He pulled his bulletproof vest off and hung it up in the coat closet. The room was silent. Nephi sat up, waiting for the next sentence. "Can we talk in the kitchen?"

Esther followed him and her mother past the fireplace and sat at the large table on the other side. The flames were visible from both sides of the fireplace and warmed the entire first floor of the house. The smell of popcorn mixed with smoke. Hart washed his hands carefully, got himself a glass of water, and sat down across the table from her with his arm draped around her mother's shoulders.

Esther still wasn't used to having a father in her life telling her what to do. Sure, it had been months since Papa J married her mom, but most of her life if she got into trouble, it was just her mom and Grandma Mable punishing her while she enthusiastically argued her case or begged for mercy—usually without success. This felt different. Quiet, not volatile. But for some strange reason, the silence created more pressure inside her gut than the family arguments she was used to. She could hear their old dog snoring in her bed in the corner. It was eerie.

Finally, Papa J leaned forward and looked her in the eyes, right to the center of her soul. "You know, Esther, one of the things I didn't count on when I fell in love with your mother was falling so deeply in love with all of you."

Esther sat back. She didn't know what to expect, but this wasn't it. She had spent all day waiting to hear how long she was grounded and how disappointed he was in her.

"I trust you, Esther. In fact, I love hanging out with you because of your wisdom and wit. I'm not surprised at all that Parker Stuart fell for you. He'd be an idiot not to."

"Is he dead? What are you trying to tell me?"

Papa J held his hand up. "Not at all. I heard from Neilson that the detectives and doctors know what's in his system. They found more in the food sent to the labs."

"What is it?" Esther sat forward. She had to know. "Is it fatal?"

"It could be. It's a lethal combination of drugs. I guess it will go out in a press release. If I tell you, you have to promise not to text it all over or share it with your friends, okay? It could cost me my job. I'm trusting you."

She nodded, but they both knew she'd tell Sophie the first chance she got.

"They found fentanyl mixed with cocaine on the candied apples. It could have been mixed in it or dusted on them while they sat on the table. Some of its street names are Murder Eight or Poison, so you can see how lethal it can be."

"Is there a cure?" Esther leaned forward. "Can they save him?"

"If there is, the doctors will know. They say if they'd known sooner, they could have used a drug for overdoses on him and maybe even prevented having to use the ventilator . . . Anyway." He shook himself like he was trying to wake up from a nightmare. "The point is, someone could have brought it to the party for recreational use, or it could have been purposely put all over the apples."

Esther sat back, thinking. "Parker would never take drugs on purpose. His dad's a doctor and his whole family cares about their health."

"Honey, there's some speculation that he could have taken the fentanyl from his dad's office. But because it's cut with some other drugs, I disagree."

"He wouldn't! I don't think I've ever even seen him go to his dad's clinic. We're both too busy with school."

"I just want you to be prepared. This is going to be a bumpy ride. You know how people gossip."

"I am. But Kohornen always gets it wrong. Sophie and I thought Jackson and Bubba had something to do with it and we aren't sure anymore." Esther stood up in frustration and started to pace back and forth in front of the sink.

"What do you mean, you were wrong? What do you know about them?"

"They're nice boys. He had prescriptions at his house, but so do lots of people. He was surprised to hear Aiden was dead. Even if it was a prank, I don't think it was on purpose."

Her mother said, "Lots of serial killers are nice guys. What does being nice mean? Sometimes it's just a show they put on."

"Yes, but I am pretty sure that isn't the case." Esther sat down and rubbed her face. *How can I explain it, so they understand?* "I know I am not a police officer or a social worker, but I have eyes and I'm pretty good at reading people. We talked honestly. It's a feeling." Esther looked at her parents and studied their faces. "But his dad?" She shrugged.

Hart leaned back in the wooden kitchen chair. He squinted at her and rubbed the noisy whiskers in his five o'clock shadow. Her mother was smiling strangely.

He took a deep breath and then blew it out slowly. He leaned forward, put his elbows on his knees, and looked into Esther's eyes. "I have more information than you do. I believe your feelings are probably valid. As a police officer, I rely on my gut daily, especially when I have to make fast decisions. But my gut has been trained by years of experience. And yet, I also remember when I was young. Maybe you're right. Maybe you're not. Are you willing to risk your life? Your friend's lives?"

The thought of being responsible for Sophie settled hard in her stomach like a rock. But her inner investigator was curious at the same time. "What do you think you know that I don't?"

"Why don't we start with what you do know?" he said.

It took several minutes for Esther to recount the day's event and their experiences. As she shared the story, she became more certain about her feelings. "Part of me wonders why Bubba would do something that would take him away from his brothers or sisters, or jeopardize his ability to care for them. You should see him with them. I go back and forth. He can become mean in a second and get seriously angry. And then I remember he got sick too. He must have eaten one of the poisoned apples. And what about Jackson? What has he got to gain? He didn't do the social media post, Bubba did. Grandma Mable always says to follow the money. There isn't any. No one gains from hurting Parker or Aiden Van Doren."

Her mother spoke for the first time. "Unless it's revenge. Did they tell you anything about how Bubba's dad and Jackson's mom died, except that they died of an overdose?"

"No." Esther shook her head. Her mother looked at her, but it was obvious she was far away, remembering something.

"Jackson's mom worked at the same gym Aiden Van Doren owns. I believe your gut is probably right," her mom said.

Surprised, Esther said, "Thank you. It . . ." Her mother held her hand up. She had more to say.

"But. This time I am asking you to trust me. Please don't go back to the trailer park alone again. Communicate with us. I don't want to have to list all the dangerous places in the world. Use your common sense. You have a cell phone and I want a text if you're unsure."

"I'm not grounded? Wait—Jackson's mom's dead too?"

Her mother chuckled and shook her head. "Yes, she is. Jackson's life has been hard. But if everyone who had a difficult childhood killed people, the world would be in a serious mess. However, a hard life doesn't excuse him, if he put something on the food on purpose or as a prank. Either way, you don't know what happened and that makes Jackson and Bubba dangerous."

Her mother and Papa J looked at each other and smiled. "Hart and I have been talking. We think grounding you and making you stay home only gives you time to complain and lie around feeling sorry for yourself, which punishes us. Instead, we'll come up with a particularly disgusting chore for you to do. No complaining. The punishment will fit the crime."

"What are you going to make me do?" Esther's heart was thumping. She was relieved and terrified all at the same time.

"We'll have to think about it. We'll let you know," Papa J said. "Now that we've handled that. Give me some popcorn, woman."

Her mother feigned shock. "Get it yourself, man!" she laughed.

He picked up a fist full of popcorn out of the bowl and threw it at her mom. She threw one back and in minutes the entire household was throwing popcorn at each other and laughing. Mary ran through the middle of the chaos, squealing in delight.

Chapter Thirteen

The Clean-Up Committee

Monday, under a gray sky, Papa J dropped Esther and Sophie off in the westside parking lot by the library. The first thing Esther noticed was yellow crime tape hanging loosely from the old doors, twisting in the autumn wind. Sophie chatted at her side while they walked up the stone steps.

"My research was conclusive. The mix of fentanyl and cocaine can be used as a street drug and has a long list of street names. But to make someone turn blue so fast, it had to be a hefty dose, and I'm convinced it was meant to do harm. Dad and I looked at the apple I brought home. That cost me. Holy cheese wiz. You should have heard the scolding I got."

"Did you get grounded?" Esther reached past the yellow tape and tried the door. As she expected, it was locked. They walked back down the steps.

"No. Anyway, after they were done scolding me for taking risks and I was done telling them that I had used a Ziplock baggie and hadn't touched anything, they were fascinated and had to look at the specimen." Sophie finally took a breath.

Esther stopped to adjust her backpack. "I did some online research in the local newspaper archives. Jackson's mother worked at Aiden Van Doren's gym. She died there of an overdose in the hot tub. There was speculation she wasn't alone, but no one was charged. She had a history of substance use."

"So that could explain why Mr. Green hates Aiden, but not why they recently were friendly enough for Aiden to invite him to come to the gym with him," Sophie said.

"Right? Clear as mud."

The bell rang loudly inside and outside of the school. Students ran for the doors.

They mounted the stairs to the doors by the office. When they pulled open the heavy double steel doors, the warm air inside hit Esther like a welcome friend. The halls were already empty. One last student breezed past them.

A heater clicked on and blew hot air down from the ceiling. Like all coasties, Esther dressed in layers. She had on a thermal shirt under her cardigan, a hoodie over that, and a down vest over that. It wasn't raining, so she'd left her raincoat home. She hoped it wasn't a mistake. She began peeling layers off while she walked, listening to Sophie talk softly.

"So, as it turns out, my parents know nothing about street drugs, so they were fascinated. They concurred with your hypothesis about the substance you mentioned. Then they were able to identify the probable amount on the apple. Speaking scientifically, it was a big enough dose to take out a bull elephant. It was definitely enough to kill. And because of the dose, the street value is massive. Maybe whoever did it had no idea how lethal it was. But it had to be someone with access to money or a substantial amount of the drug."

"Street value?" Esther asked.

"You know. What the dealer charges for the drug. I researched the sale of illegal substances as well."

"Sophie, take a look. Let's go talk to Bridget in the office." Esther nodded in the direction of Principal Kelly's office. His office was entirely surrounded by glass. They had once put the glass in for the safety of the students, so that no leader or teacher would ever be alone in a closed room with a student. But the unexpected consequence was that everyone saw you when you were getting in trouble.

Ms. Priest, the librarian, sat in front of Mr. Kelly's desk with tears and makeup running down her pale face. Her normally pale nose was bright red. Mr. Kelly sat on the corner of his desk over her with his back to the girls. They couldn't hear what he was saying, but whatever it was it was making Ms. Priest cry. He reached out and touched her shoulder. Ms. Priest jerked away, reached for a Kleenex box on the desk and blew her nose.

"Crepes. What is he saying to her?" Sophie asked.

"I don't know but let's get closer."

The girls went into the office, where their friend Bridget worked on attendance during first period.

Esther leaned against the chest-high counter. Sophie was so short only her eyes were above the counter. Bridget looked up from what she was working on and they locked eyes. Bridget's eyes shifted towards Ms. Priest and then got large.

"What's going on?" Esther asked softly.

"How can I help you?" Bridget said loudly. Esther noticed Ms. Priest's head snap up. The talk in the next office got softer.

Then Bridget lowered her voice and whispered. "I don't know what's going on, but your friend Ironpot just dropped her off and came in to tell Mr. Kelly they were done in the library, so we could clean it up. Mr. Kelly saw him with Ms. Priest, and so he called her into his office. He sounded really firm. Something about a drug test and then she started to cry, and he got quiet."

Sophie stood on her tiptoes and asked, "Did you hear who they plan to drug test?"

Bridget shrugged. "I'm not sure."

"How does he know about the drugs? The paper hasn't come out yet," Esther said.

Bridget shrugged. "It's a small town."

"We don't want to embarrass her," Esther said. "Do you know if we can get into the library? Are the police still in there or can we get a key from the office?"

Esther's phone dinged loudly. Mr. Kelly stuck his head out of the office door and said, "Turn that phone off, Miss James, unless you want me to take it away from you."

Esther turned the ringer off on her phone, but it continued to vibrate over and over, so she scurried out of the office with Sophie on her heels.

"Who is it? Man. They text a lot."

"It's a group text. You're in it."

"My phone is on silent, for school." Sophie fished her phone out of her pack, and they rounded the corner where they could read the texts without being seen.

> Paisley to Nephi, Sophie, Esther, and Bridget: *Parker opened his eyes! He is still intubated, but I think it's a good sign. For a minute anyway. We are hopeful!!! Prayers k?*
> Text from Nephi: **Prayer hand emoji* There at noon. He's got this. *Clapping hand emojis**
> Text from Bridget: **Hug emoji* *prayer hands emoji.* So happy!*
> Text from Sophie: *I never doubted. Now let's get the jerk that did this to him.*
> Text from Esther: *XOXO Tell him we love him.*

Tears started running down Esther's face. She held her shaking hand over her mouth and tried to cry silently, but she finally took a jagged breath in and then sank to her knees. Sophie knelt beside her and held her for a moment while all her fears ran in rivers to the floor.

Her phone vibrated in her hand again and she pulled the phone back from her chest to see, through tears, a photo of Parker with tubes in his mouth, and an IV in his arm. His eyes were open and looking wildly at the camera. A nurse was in the background shooting something into the IV.

The photo didn't make her feel any better.

Moments later, in the girl's bathroom, Esther splashed cold water on her blotchy face. Then Sophie handed her little squares of toilet paper so she could blow her nose.

"I'm going to get a key from the janitor and get into the library." Sophie shook her head as Esther blew her nose loudly. The long bathroom had an antique metal sink for handwashing that was round and stood in the center of the room. You put your foot on a pedal and water sprayed out of all sides, dropping gracefully into the sink. Esther kept her foot on the pedal and splashed handful after handful of icy water on her face.

Sophie pushed the heavy wooden door open just far enough to look down the hall. Empty. She pushed it open a little further and checked the other direction. "All clear." She motioned for Esther to follow her.

Esther pulled a paper towel out of the metal dispenser on the wall and dried her face. She realized the entire front of her brown hoodie was wet, but she didn't care.

Simon, the janitor, knew the girls worked in the library, even when Ms. Priest wasn't in school. They found him in the broom closet loading up a mop bucket. He led the way to the inside library doors, and using keys on a chain clipped to his belt, let the girls in.

The room was dark and disheveled. It was like walking into a time capsule from one of the worst moments of Esther's life. She could see herself busy with Sophie and Ms. Priest, so focused on the stupid punch and food that she hadn't paid enough attention to Parker. They never really got to talk. *Why was I so upset about little things? Maybe if I danced with him when he asked, he wouldn't have had time to eat the candy or drink the punch.*

"Yikes. I know it's a mess, but before we clean it up, we need to look for clues." Sophie switched on the light by the door when Ms. Priest passed her silently. She went into her office and sat down without turning the lights on.

They looked at each other and quietly sat down in her dark office.

"What was that all about?" Esther asked.

Ms. Priest shook her head and squeezed her eyes tightly shut. She took a few slow and steady breaths, squared her shoulders, and stood up. "I suppose you girls saw the news."

It wasn't really a question, so Esther didn't reply.

"First, the police interrogated me like I had killed Aiden and poisoned Parker. This morning they searched my house. Ironpot dropped me off, because my car was in the parking lot here, and he has to search it too. Then, because I was dating Aiden, Mr. Kelly says he is required by the school board to ask me to take a drug test. But Principal Kelly says he is on my side and can help me." She closed her eyes for a second, took a deep breath, opened her eyes, picked her lamp up off the floor and put it back on her desk. She reached under the Tiffany glass shade and turned it on. Quietly, the girls helped her pick up the books on the floor and put them back on the shelf behind her desk.

"Is there anything we can do?" Esther asked.

She shook her head. "I can't think about it all or I won't make it through the day." She gave them a weak smile.

Sophie leapt to her feet. "I can't stop thinking about it. I can't believe the police suspected you or that the school board would think you use drugs."

"My dad hired an attorney for me," Ms. Priest sighed.

"I am so sorry this happened to you," Esther said. Ms. Priest gave her a quick hug and a sad smile.

Sophie frowned. "I'm not just sorry. I am furious. We're going to figure out what happened even if the police don't."

"The police sure made a mess when they searched the library," Esther said.

"Well, I think Principal Kelly is a coward." Sophie adjusted her round glasses on her face, filled with determination. "I think the test is his idea, and he is treating you more like a student than a teacher. I think he's mad that you liked Aiden and not him."

Ms. Priest chuckled. "Believe it or not, sometimes being a grown-up is hard too. And adults can often be treated like kids by employers. Of course, I want the principal to trust me. He's right. If something else happens, and he hasn't tested me, the parents would want his head and mine. I have to go to the local testing site at noon."

"I thought they already arrested Bubba and Jackson," Esther said.

"They were leaving the police station. I saw Mr. Green pick them up late last night." Ms. Priest shook her head again as she used a cleaning wipe from her desk drawer to dust all the surfaces. "You're students. You shouldn't worry about all this stuff."

"We care about you, and we need to make sure Parker or even one of the rest of the student body or faculty wasn't the intended target," Esther said.

"Fair enough. I agree. We also have to make sure no one else is ever hurt again."

"What do you mean, again?" Sophie asked.

Ms. Priest bit her lip and then dove in. "I don't think anyone who could do such a random and dangerous thing will do it just once. I think we all need to watch our backs."

"I agree." Esther nodded. "Was your dad with you?"

"My dad wasn't there. They wouldn't allow it. He knows how I feel, or I guess felt about Aiden. It was the round-faced detective, Kohornen."

"So Kohornen questioned you?" Sophie asked.

"Yes, and just as usual, he thinks he knows the answers before he asks the questions. He said he was sure Aiden and Parker were friends and probably met at the gym and were using together. He wanted to know if I had seen anything or knew anything about Aiden using substances. I also heard he thinks Parker had it first and either spiked Aiden's food or shared it with him. He asked if Parker had a reason to kill Aiden. Can you believe that?"

"Wait a minute," Esther said. "Are you saying Parker is a suspect? That doesn't make any sense at all. What would be his motive?" Esther's voice rose several levels as panic set in. "I'm going to call Papa J. How can they be so dense?" Her blood was boiling.

"Wait!" Ms. Priest held her hand up. "I'm not sure I'm supposed to know all of that. I overheard some of it. The walls between the interrogation rooms are thin. I heard them talking to Jackson about it. For some reason, they thought he would know about what Aiden and Parker were doing. They kept him longer and were grilling him about his dad and why he fought with Aiden. Do you remember the secret he said he had during their fight?"

"Well, we should warn Paisley that they are looking at Parker as a suspect and searching houses," Sophie said.

"Okay. But they aren't going to find a thing. I promise you." Esther rearranged the chairs and stepped back. "There. At least your office is in order."

"Girls, I don't want you to do anything out in the main library. What if that awful drug is still here somewhere, like on the furniture?"

"Don't you think they would have found evidence of the drugs when they had the crime scene investigators in here?" Sophie turned on the main library lights.

Esther sighed. "I have no clue. We can wear gloves. We'll be here when you get back from your test. I don't have any classes until fourth period and I can try to get excused if we aren't done." Esther surveyed the damage. The room looked like the party had ended in a brawl. Twinkle lights still hung from the ceiling. Sound equipment and cords were everywhere, and no one had cleaned up the vomit on the floor. "Do you think we should call Simon, the janitor?"

Ms. Priest pulled a cell phone out of her pocket. "I'll text him. He has to take care of all bodily fluid spills with special chemicals. But earlier he said we should throw away all the books that were in the area of the dance. I get nervous about what he thinks of as cleaning. Keep an eye on Simon when he arrives. I don't want him to toss any books until I look at them."

The library door opened, and Principal Kelly came into the library and stood looking down and not making eye contact at the main desk.

"Cynnomon," he said, using her first name. "Can we talk?"

"Come into my office," Ms. Priest held the door opened. Without looking up, he entered the office and sat in one of the chairs facing her desk."

Esther and Sophie looked at each other.

"Let's listen," Sophie said.

Esther's eyebrows raised and her mouth fell opened. "Seriously?"

"We'll just stand casually outside the glass door, so she knows we're here."

"You're right the door is glass, but because it's glass, he'll see us," Esther said.

"Okay, you stay here, and I'll listen." Sophie marched past the glass door. Once she was out of sight, she leaned against the wall, near the door.

"Oh, alright." Esther joined Sophie and listened in. The door was glass, but it was thick enough she could only catch phrases and words.

Principal Kelly said, "Not a date. You need to be taken care of . . . Cynnomon, I . . ."

Esther peeked around the corner. Ms. Priest was weeping again, but without expression. She sat up straight in her chair, hands on her desk, scowling.

"Let me help you with the board . . ." Principal Kelly leaned over the desk and she sat back in her chair.

"Thank you for the offer," Cynnomon said.

Principal Kelly stood up quickly enough that his chair almost fell over. He caught it and turned to go to the door.

"Move," Esther said, and ran past Sophie for the stacks. Sophie passed her, and they hid behind the shelf before the glass door opened.

"Thank you for your offer, but I don't mix work and my personal life," Cynnomon said.

He turned to leave, his back to Esther. He looked over his shoulder, scowled, and pushed his way out of the library. Ms. Priest wiped something invisible off one arm and then the other. She sighed loudly.

"Girls," Ms. Priest said, "I need to run to take the test. If you can wait for me, I would like to talk to you about the haunted house today. I would appreciate it."

Simon, the janitor, came into the library with a mop in a bucket and a cart full of cleaning supplies.

"Simon, I have to run up to the clinic for a minute. The girls know what needs to be done. Girls, would you show Simon where everything goes while he works, and I'll be back soon." She went back into her office, took her large black satchel from below her desk, and put on a jacket.

The girls watched her walk sadly out the west library doors, tearing away the yellow tape as she went.

"I wonder what she wants us to do to help with the haunted house?" Sophie said.

"I have no clue, but I say we surprise her and get this place shipshape before she returns," Esther said.

"Agreed. And while we're at it, we look for clues."

The janitor moved his cleaning cart with a squeaky wheel closer to the front desk. "Hey. Isn't that your boyfriend's car? The one in the hospital? Green is outside towing it?" He pointed over his shoulder.

Esther and Sophie dashed for the door. Mr. Green was at Parker's black BMW. It was still where Parker had left it on the night of the dance when he left in an ambulance. Mr. Green was by the driver's door. "What is he doing? Is he trying to get into it?" Esther asked.

"I don't know. But I'm going to lash myself to the hood to keep him from towing it."

They rushed through the cars to where the truck and car were parked side by side near the road. Mr. Green's back was to them, and he seemed to be wrestling with something at the driver's door.

"Hey! Hey!" Sophie yelled, waving her small but mighty arm. Her black hair flying in the wind. "Get away from that car!"

His head snapped up and he turned suspiciously and then turned his back to them and stuck a bright orange sticker on the windshield.

"This is Parker Stuart's car." Esther was breathing hard after the sprint. "You know, the boy in the hospital. The family that gave you money?"

"Who told you that?" Spittle flew out of Mr. Green's mouth, and chewing tobacco dribbled down his whiskered chin. He wiped it off with the back of a greasy hand. "That arrangement was 'tween us. I'm helping him out by towing his son's car back to their house, so they don't need to pick it up. I appreciate Mr. Stuart and want to help him whenever he needs it."

"Do you have permission because this car is legally parked," Sophie barked.

Esther frantically texted Paisley: *Does Mr. Green have your family's permission to tow Parker's car? He's here now.*

The reply from Paisley was quick: *No.*

Paisley's text was followed by a pic shot of both her parents at Parker's bedside and another text: *I asked.*

"You do not have anyone's permission to tow this car," Esther said firmly.

"How do you know, little missy?" He spit chew onto the road at her feet, spattering on her black suede boots.

"I asked." Esther held up the phone so he could see the pic and text stream.

"The sticker stays. Student cars aren't to be parked overnight. Move it or lose it. I'm calling the principal." He climbed the ladder to get into the lifted truck and shut the door. The motor idled and Esther saw him making a call.

"Let's go back in, E. It's cold."

Esther realized that black clouds had rolled in, making the air smell of rain. She knew what it meant. When she reached the stone steps, her suspicions were confirmed. Small hail pellets stung as they hit her nose and face. They dashed inside the door just in time to see the entire parking lot and the waiting student vehicles turn white as if it had snowed.

"Look who's pulling in." Esther pointed. The hale stopped as abruptly as it started. Angelica Rose had pulled in, driving what appeared to be a brand new SUV being pelted by hail. She parked beside Green, driver's window to driver's window. The hail slowed and stopped abruptly. Nevaeh got out of the passenger side door, carrying her backpack. Her face was so pale, Esther thought she looked almost gray, and her clothes hung on her like a hanger.

Ms. Rose got out of the car. She was wearing her matching jogging suit. She got closer to the truck. Mr. Green rolled down his window and they talked. Esther wanted to go outside so she could hear what they were talking about, but Nevaeh was coming to the library doors.

Nevaeh was blocking their view. When she opened the library doors, Esther heard Angelica yelling at Green, but she couldn't make out the words. She got back in her SUV and sped off.

Esther quickly texted Paisley, letting her know they might try to search the house or cars. Her reply was simply, *let them.*

Nevaeh followed the girls back inside. "Mom's gone to get a coffee for herself and Ms. Priest. She said she would bring us hot chocolate. She's anxious to get her candy trays back and cleaned up."

"How's she doing?" Sophie asked. "She looked really upset, almost angry." Sophie raised one eyebrow above her round glasses and tilted her head as she gathered withering pumpkins from the floor by the door.

"She hates Mr. Green. I don't know why. Every time he passes us, she looks like that. Who knows?" Nevaeh sounded tired, like exploding was a daily event. She shrugged. "I'll go to the janitor's closet and see if I can find a bigger garbage can or even larger bags. We'll need it for the pumpkins, tree branches, and leaves. I'll find out what dumpster he wants us to use for all this garbage."

"Hey, Nevaeh," Esther said. "You sound so tired. Are you okay?"

"Yeah. Honestly, I am probably just sad about Aiden, I mean Mr. Van Doren. I feel like I must be bad luck. Everyone I really like dies."

"You're not bad luck. I think everyone is sad that he died, and that Parker is sick," Esther said.

Esther watched Sophie melt, but only for a moment. One of Sophie's eyebrows raised like a thermometer for a hot idea. She stepped closer to Nevaeh. "Have you had any other gastrointestinal symptoms? Bluish lips? Trouble breathing? How are your nasal passages?"

Nevaeh chuckled, "Well, Dr. Sophie. If I did eat any poison, I threw it up all over the highway and left it long behind me. But . . ." She blushed. "Thanks for caring about me."

Esther couldn't help herself. She reached out and hugged Nevaeh. She realized she felt unusually thin. Nevaeh had always carried a little weight. She had often done her "junk in the trunk" dance to make the kids laugh. Esther let go and stepped back. The dark circles under Nevaeh's eyes had become ever present. "Are you feeling okay? Sophie's right. How's Nevaeh?"

"I've had a constant stomachache and nausea since the dance, but it's getting better. I feel like it's just anxiety. You know, the stress of the whole thing. But I'm fine, really. Let's get this mess cleaned up."

The west doors opened, and River Peace poked his head into the library. "Hello? Anybody home?"

River waved at the girls from the doorway. "I'm just coming to get my equipment. I heard the police were through with it."

Esther was caught off guard and hesitated.

Nevaeh smiled at him. "Before you start loading, let me get past you and take this garbage bag of rotten pumpkins out." Sophie opened the door for her. Nevaeh looked over her shoulder and said, "I'll be back after I toss these into the dumpster and find more bags."

"The police are done.," Sophie said as he came into the library. "They haven't done a thing, but they're done all right. You might as well destroy the rest of the evidence."

"Thanks." River pulled a plug from the wall.

"But," Sophie said. "Before you do, I would like to take pictures of the dance floor and sound equipment where the victim was located at the time of his death." She took her cell out of her pocket and took a snap of River.

Esther couldn't tell if he was surprised or not, because as usual his eyes were hidden behind sunglasses.

River's long, droopy mustache lifted a bit. "Cheese."

Esther stifled a giggle while Sophie took multiple photos of the equipment, dance floor, and River as he took various poses. If he hadn't been wearing a sheepskin vest over a paisley shirt and leather pants, he would have looked like a model on the catwalk.

"You really should take this more seriously." Sophie moved in for a close up of the cords and the floor.

"Why? The paper says we don't even have a murder. The chief is quoted as saying that this may just be a case of a bad party. It'll be filed away as an accidental overdose during recreational drug use. An officer told me that one of the possibilities is your boyfriend, Parker, spiked the food and got more than he bargained for. I heard they're also exploring other students who may have been angry. The officer also said they have what they need, so I can take my equipment home," River said.

Once again, Esther felt her fury rise. Hearing Parker talked about as a drug addict, or even someone who was willing to experiment, infuriated her. "You don't know Parker. He would never do anything like that. And Mr. Van Doren was into working out. Why would he use something that could harm him?"

"Well, well, little miss. You should ask the other gym rats. He was never afraid of a little juice, if you get my drift."

"Juice?" Esther asked.

"Check it out with your new pop. He'll tell you. Everyone knows his crowd juices. And if you buy one thing from a guy, why not buy another?"

"Do you know who the person is that sells juice?" The wheels in Esther's mind were spinning. *Who sells drugs in this town? And if he takes juice or uses steroids, maybe . . .?*

River stood up and said, "Juice. You buy it at low tide."

"What? What does the tide have to do with juice?"

River just cackled and kept putting away equipment.

Sophie was videotaping River rolling up his cords and Sophie watched the scene play out when Esther tapped Sophie on the shoulder. She motioned for Sophie to follow her.

When they reached Ms. Priest's office, she pulled Sophie in and shut the door. "I've got an idea."

"Can't it wait?"

"Forget River. He isn't motivated enough to take a bath more than once a week. He isn't the one who . . . we have to find."

"Okay," Sophie said. "What's your idea?"

"If we find the drug dealer, we can push them to tell us who bought the fentanyl and cocaine. We'll be able to figure out who the killer is and who poisoned Parker. They should be one of the people who bought the drugs, or the dealer." Esther waited while Sophie thought for a minute.

Slowly, Sophie smiled. "I like it. Do you want to start at the private gym Parker goes to? After we clean up this mess for Ms. Priest. Suddenly I am hungry again. We're going to find out who hurt Parker, I know it."

"I hate throwing all this food away. These cookies haven't been touched. Do you want some?" Nevaeh asked.

"Maybe. But eating food here makes me nervous." Sophie left the office.

Ms. Priest was coming towards the counter just as Esther reached the cookies.

Ms. Priest picked the plate up and dumped the contents into the garbage. "I don't think I'll ever be hungry again. That drug test was the most humiliating thing I have ever had to do."

Angelica Rose returned with to-go trays of coffee and hot chocolate. She slid in the door just before River Peace carried a six-foot-tall black speaker out to his purple VW van. "Nevaeh. Shouldn't you be in class?"

Nevaeh was busy throwing away flowers and paper decorations. "I don't feel like school."

"Nonsense. Life gives us lemons. We make lemon curd." Angelica crossed the room to Ms. Priest. "I bought the girls some hot chocolate and brought you a coffee. Out in the car, I have a pot of homemade chicken soup, dear. I ordered it from Posh and Sandy."

Ms. Priest smiled with her mouth. Her eyes remained flat. "Thanks."

Sophie said softly to Esther, "I bet she tosses the soup too."

"Cynnomon," Angelica said sweetly. "Why don't you go home and let us take care of all of this." She held her hands out and motioned around the room.

"Thanks. But being busy keeps my mind off things. I'm sure you're as upset as I am. I also need to fill the girls in on the booster club's haunted house. We're going to need their help."

"Then go to your office and I will bring you some soup." Angelica put an arm around Ms. Priest and led her into her office. She pulled the door closed and left through the double doors.

Ding.

> Text to Esther from Paisley: *How are you doing? This is awful.*
>
> Text to Paisley: *Will they let us see him?*
>
> Text to Esther: *No. Dr. Satchel says family only, and there is now an officer napping in a chair outside the room.*
>
> Text to Paisley: *What?! Why???*
>
> Text to Esther: *I am not sure. Watching him? Safety? Or because he is a suspect? I should be glad, but it infuriates me.*
>
> Text to Paisley: *We miss you. We will find out who did this.*

Sophie was looking over her shoulder. "And then only heaven can save that person."

Esther shook her head and smiled at Sophie. "What are we going to do? Scream them to death? Restrain him with my cardigan?"

Nevaeh snickered. Esther realized she must have been listening. *Here's our chance to learn more. What if she was mad enough to spike Aiden's food and Parker was hurt on accident?*

"Who do you think might have poisoned Aiden, Nevaeh?" Esther tried to sound casual.

"I don't know. He was nice for a while, but then he really hurt my mom. Maybe he upset someone besides my mom."

"What do you mean when you say for a while?" Esther asked.

"I really miss the fun we had. He was like a dad. I liked having him around until he changed. It felt like he got mad for no reason."

"What did he say when he was angry?" Sophie asked.

"He just complained about mom's business being a waste of money."

"I thought he had his own money?" Esther said.

Nevaeh shrugged. "I guess. I told him our money comes from a trust in my name and we could use it as we liked. After that, things were different. He slammed doors and yelled. But, I still wanted to fix things, you know? I told him if he stayed with Mom, he would have the candy shop too, you know? Things seemed to be better for a day or two, but then we had the meeting and well, he was with Ms. Priest."

"The money is in your name?" Sophie put down the broom and said, "All of it?"

"Well, what's left of my dad's life insurance policy. I think he thought there was a lot more money left, but we used it to buy the sweet shop, and to pay living expenses."

Esther pulled the library cart out from behind the main desk. "Did he break up with your mom because she doesn't have enough money?"

Nevaeh used gloves, a rag, and bleach water to wipe the table they had used for refreshments. "Maybe. I heard her tell him it takes money to make money, and then they argued. After that, we didn't see him the entire week before the committee meeting. I don't understand at all. After all, Aiden had way more than we did. He gave Mom her SUV a few weeks before they broke up. She calls it her 'consolation prize.'"

"Your mom must make money at her shops. They're always packed." Sophie put on a second set of gloves and began picking library books up and wiping them down. She stacked them for Esther, who sorted them onto a cart to return to the shelves.

"She does okay."

"How old were you when your dad died?" Esther asked casually.

"I was nine. I was twelve when Angelica got married to someone else." Nevaeh smiled. "He was great. He taught me how to fly."

"How did you lose him?" Esther asked.

"His plane fell apart in the air over the California Desert just before we moved here. We sold the California house to put a down payment on the first sweetshop. We still live above it. I love our little apartment. The money he left mom got us through a few years while the business grew. We're fine."

"Nevaeh, I wasn't fine when my world fell apart. You don't have to be fine." Esther smiled, set down her books, took a rag out of the bleach water, and began trying to scrub the tape marks off the old table. "I was sure I wanted to just disappear."

Nevaeh stopped wiping but didn't look up. "Honestly, I have terrible anxiety whenever I think about losing someone else. It makes it really hard to even get close to Mom. I mean, even though she has always been there for me, I have all this fear about being hurt if she leaves me. It's hard to explain."

Sophie dumped a pile of books on the cart and fell into a chair by the table. "Who wouldn't have anxiety after all that—or just after this week. We need some serious girl time."

"Girl time?" Esther's eyebrows raised, and she tried not to laugh.

"You know. Go to the big city library. Oh! Or that new bookstore in Cabbott's Cove."

"Whoa. Slow down there, wild woman." Nevaeh laughed. "What are you going to do to wrap up your day? Go to a poetry reading?" She laughed so hard she snorted, and some light returned to her eyes.

"Laugh it up. Have you got any better ideas in this wild and crazy town?" Sophie said.

"Anything is better than a quiet library. Pizza and the arcade or the hot tub at the pool. Oh! I know, we could have a party."

The door to Ms. Priest's office opened. "Girls, do you have a minute?"

They put down their cleaning tools and joined her in her office.

Ms. Priest remained standing behind the desk. "As you know, the school boosters club has partnered with student leadership to do a haunted house at the old canning factory on the dock. It's a fundraiser for students in need. Paisley was in charge of getting students to help with the house and help the boosters decorate."

Esther's mouth fell open and she sat down in a chair. "Are we still having it? After everything that's happened?"

"I asked Principal Kelly the very same question," Ms. Priest said. "He met with the boosters in a phone conference and they all feel getting back to normal and having something to look forward to would be good for the students."

Sophie pushed her glasses up her nose and folded her arms. "Then why do I feel like I'm watching Psycho and need to shout, 'Don't take a shower?'" Sophie said.

"Believe me, I feel the same way. I even called my dad at the police station," Ms. Priest said. "He promised that he, your stepdad, Esther, and other officers would attend and make sure everyone was safe."

"We could refuse to do it," Esther said.

Mrs. Priest sat on the edge of her desk and cleared her throat. "I don't want to push my luck right now. Look, I understand if you don't want to help. You don't have to."

"I'll help," Sophie said.

"Would you?" She looked back and forth between the two faces in the room.

Esther looked at Sophie, who nodded. Esther nodded and said, "Of course. What should we do first?"

"Tomorrow, we'll sign students up in the library to volunteer. We need volunteers to decorate and set up the event. I would ask that we cancel it, but we're raising funds for student's family's sports fees and canned food for the local food bank for Thanksgiving."

"We're on it," Esther said. "I'll get all the information I can from Paisley when she texts me and the time feels right."

"Oh, thank you. I knew I could count on you. You two have already lost an entire day of classes helping me clean up. Let's close this place up and start again in the morning. I am exhausted." She smiled, but it came across as more sad than happy. She pulled a stray hair off her face and went back into her office.

"It's settled, Nevaeh. You're helping us with the haunted house on Saturday," Esther said. "It will be the wildest party this town has ever seen."

"It actually sounds fun. I am sure Mom will help because she is a member of the boosters. But right now, she thinks I need a weekend mental health makeover. I doubt she'll let me go."

Angelica Rose came back through the double doors carrying a stack of cookie sheets, serving trays, and a punch bowl. "Nevaeh. Open the door. Help me load these into the car. Girls, do you need a ride home? I'm headed that way and it's absolutely beastly out there."

Esther shook her head, no. "We'll call Grandma Mable for a ride, since it's raining, but thank you. You go ahead. We'll help Ms. Priest lock up."

Chapter Fourteen

The Cast and Crew

Esther and Sophie waited inside the library doors until Mable and Nephi pulled up outside and honked. The rain was coming down so hard that in the time they ran from the library doors to the car, they were drenched.

"Thanks, Grandma. Want a wet hug?" Esther said.

"No! How goes the investigation?" Mable turned around to look at them in the back seat and raised one brow. When they didn't respond, she laughed. "That good?"

"People are saying it was an overdose. Everyone else thinks that Bubba and Jackson had something to do with it. And we're not sure they didn't," Esther said.

"Yeah, and we can't figure out who else has a motive," Sophie said.

"Exactly," Mable answered. "Who stands to gain?"

"No one at all," Esther said. "None of it makes any sense. Nevaeh's mom was mad that Aiden left her, but Nevaeh says they don't have much money."

"Not much money?" Mable asked. "If they have four sweet shops that are owned and if each one is busy as we know they are, they could be worth a tidy sum. Their shop is on is prime property in Cabbot's cove. I would say the shops are worth a few million alone. There's poor and then there's poor because I have all my money tied up in investments. That isn't poor like you think. It's all relative."

"I guess you're right. I was just telling Jackson the same thing," Esther said.

"Don't forget Nevaeh. She was accused of setting the fire that killed her father before Angelica adopted her," Sophie added.

"She's adopted?" Mable asked.

"Yes. Not only that, Nevaeh's father was killed in a fire and her stepfather, Angelica's husband, was killed in a plane crash," Esther said. "I'm getting online and finding out more about the deaths."

"Both men are dead? That's interesting. But what would Angelica's motive be? They were already broken up," Mable said. "Who are your other suspects?" She looked at the girls in the side mirror while heading home. "And who wants hot chocolate from Sea Beach Coffee Shack?"

Nephi perked up. "Can I have a double and a muffin?"

"Sure," Mable smiled at her boy. "Now, Esther, who gains by Aiden's death, or was he the target?"

"That's just it," Esther said. "We haven't got a clue. Everyone thought it was Bubba after his post threatening to burn the school down, but now we have our doubts. Mr. Green threatened to tell a secret he had and almost blackmailed Aiden with it. Then Aiden gave him back his truck and Jackson doesn't know why. Honestly, we're not even sure who the target was, or if it was just some random cruel joke."

"It was seriously not funny, if it was a joke," Sophie said. "I have another question. Where do you get a street drug that lethal, Mable?"

"I don't," Mable chuckled.

Esther turned toward Sophie. "You're right. If it was a joke, it was seriously not funny. We asked River Peace where people bought drugs, and he said you could only buy them at low tide. What kind of answer is that?"

Nephi chucked in the front seat. "It's a River Peace answer. He had too much fun in the seventies."

"Now, now," Mable said. "Are you sure?"

"Of course I am, aren't you?"

Mable didn't answer. The Sea Beach Shack was on Highway 101, just past the edge of town. The walls were cedar shingles and surfboards hung on every side. Mable pulled up to the drive-through window and idled.

The window slid open and Janet, a senior at their school, leaned out. "Hi, Nephi." She grinned coyly.

"Hey, Janet."

Sophie poked Esther in the ribs, looked at her, and rolled her eyes.

"I haven't seen you here before. You should come here more often. Is this your mom?"

Nephi sat up straighter and combed his hair with his fingers, smiling in her direction.

"Oh, good grief." Sophie kicked the back of his seat.

"Hi Janet," Mable said. "We would love four of your biggest hot chocolates, with whip cream, a muffin, and a child's size hot chocolate to go." She looked at Esther in the rearview mirror. "Mary is home with your mom. She'll be sad if she doesn't get one."

Janet looked over her shoulder and bellowed at a girl behind her, "Four chocolates, whipped, one child's and the best muffin we have." She turned back around and her smile magically reappeared. Nephi smiled back at her. She didn't say another word. She just kept posing and smiling in the window.

"Did you just flex your muscles?" Sophie kicked his seat hard. Without looking back, he reached over into the back and grabbed her foot. The smile never left his face.

"Are you going to the haunted house?" Janet asked Nephi.

Mable pulled her head back and looked at him with one raised eyebrow.

"I have to help with it. Are you going?"

"Let go of my foot." Sophie kicked the seat with her other foot.

Janet began passing hot chocolates and the muffin out to the car. "I hope I see you there." She finally looked at Mable and gave her the price. "Do you want to leave a tip?"

"Yes. If you're going to be nice, be nice to the person with the money." Mable took her change and drove away.

"Mom!" Nephi let go of Sophie's ankle and slouched in his seat.

"Back to the problem at hand," Grandma Mable said. "Where does someone get the drugs used to poison Aiden, Parker, and Bubba?"

"We have no leads. Low tide doesn't help us at all," Esther said.

"Doesn't it?" Grandma Mable asked. She stopped the car on the side of the highway just inside of town.

"Where are we?" Sophie asked.

Mable didn't say a word. She just pointed out the window. They were outside a notoriously rowdy bar. The doors were closed, and the windows were all blacked out, but somehow the music still made it to the full parking lot.

A shabby sign over the door was barely readable. It said, "Low Tide."

"Low Tide is the bar!" Sophie sat on the edge of her seat.

"And look," Esther said, "There's Green's tow truck."

"Hold my hot chocolate, Nephi." Mable took her keys and opened the car door.

"Mom, you can't go in there. This place is gross."

"Watch me."

Nephi groaned, put his hands over his eyes, and slid further down in his seat.

"How long has she been in there? I have to go to the bathroom," Sophie said.

"Forever." Nephi rolled down his window and some of the steam on the glass dissipated.

"It's only been a half-hour or so. I'm going to go check out Green's truck." Esther opened her door.

"Don't do anything dumb." Nephi sat up. "Esther."

She shut the door and walked across the gravel parking lot to the large green truck. She walked around it to the passenger's side door and climbed up on the running board, holding onto the rearview mirror to get a look inside. It was spotless. Not a sheet of paper or even a pop bottle in the cab. It had a locked armrest and container between the seats and a locked glove box.

She tried the door. Locked.

"Are you crazy?" Sophie growled.

Startled, Esther's heart leapt. She jumped down and whispered, "You scared me to death!"

"What are you doing going out here all alone? Did you try the door?"

"Yeah. It's locked."

The entrance to the Low Tide opened and two women came out cackling with Grandma Mable. "You girls have a good night now! Don't do anything this old grandma wouldn't. And if you do, come fetch me!" The women broke into louder laughter and then got into their car and drove away while Mable waved like she was flagging down a trucker on the interstate.

She swaggered back to the Jeep, where the girls met her.

"What kind of accent was that?" Sophie asked.

"That's the 'I'm your best bar buddy' accent." Mable chuckled.

"Did it work? What did you learn?" Esther said.

"Mr. Green is selling the very drugs we're looking for. And my new friends buy one of them regularly. All they have to do is call for a tow. Come on, let's go home and make another murder board on the garage wall. Fill me in on the way."

Esther opened the garage door. Turning on the lights, she realized Parker had left one of his sweatshirts on the driver's seat in the van. She picked it up and buried her face in it. It smelled like him, wonderful. Missing him, she pulled it over her shirt and wrapped herself in the warmth of his scent.

"Stop moping, E." Sophie smacked Esther on the back, waking her up. After sending a text to Paisley asking about Parker, she found a marker for the wall.

Grandma Mable came out and put a plate of cookies and soda pop on the tool bench. "Dinner is served."

"You're the best grandmother on earth," Sophie said. She took a cookie in each hand.

"Thanks, Mom," Nephi said. He took three and sat on the rolling chair and leaned on the van.

"Don't dent the door," Sophie said. Nephi leaned forward with his elbows on his knees eating his second cookie.

"I'll get the Diet Coke," He went to the fridge, put a six pack on the tool bench and took two.

Esther drew a circle in the center of the board and wrote *Aiden* in it. She drew a circle of equal size next to it and wrote *Parker*. Then she drew another circle and wrote *Jackson and Bubba*. "After asking around school and checking social media, these are the people we know either were affected by the drugs at the party or in Bubba's case—may have been affected."

"Jackson and Bubba did it to get back at me," Nephi said and frowned. "Parker is probably in the hospital because of my fight at school."

"I am not sure about Jackson. Bubba could have done it on his own, like the social media post," Esther said. "But after going to Jackson's house, he just doesn't feel like a killer. He's more likely to go paint a picture about his feelings, if you ask me."

"Do you really believe Jackson didn't know about Bubba posting the picture?" Nephi asked. "Girls. You go all gooey over a guy because he's cute or nice. Maybe he didn't mean to actually kill anyone."

"We can't rule him out, I guess," Esther said.

"Nephi's right. He is cute but we should keep Jackson on the wall. Spiking the punch is normal . . ." Sophie looked at Mable and cleared her throat, "But completely unacceptable high school boy behavior. What about Nevaeh?" Sophie asked.

"Good question. She is sick, but she says it's something else. What do you think?" Esther said.

"Just put her on the wall with a note that she is ill—unknown origins. What would her motive be?" Mable pulled out a lawn chair and sat facing the wall, thinking.

"Nevaeh may have been targeting Aiden for leaving her mom and dating Ms. Priest. You know—revenge. Jackson and Bubba might have been targeting Nephi for getting them into trouble or just random students. Jackson may have had access to the drugs his dad was selling." She wrote drugs and Mr. Green on the board. "Mr. Green certainly hated Aiden for repossessing his truck, but by the dance he had it back. Wait . . . when Mr. Green was yelling at Aiden while we decorated, he said that he had given Aiden what he wanted. River said the body builders used drugs like steroids. Maybe Mr. Green sold drugs to Aiden?"

"That's a great point," Sophie said. "What if he told Aiden he was giving him steroids, but they were actually the drugs that killed him? Aiden could have taken them thinking they were something he had been taking."

"So, Mr. Green needs to stay on the wall too. He sounded like he was blackmailing Aiden. But we can't prove any of that," Esther said.

"But Mr. Green wasn't at the dance. How would he have poisoned Parker?" Grandma Mable asked.

Esther tapped the marker against her leg. "He was in the parking lot and talking to kids. He could have sent it in with someone or gone in the library when it was empty after we decorated and before the dance started. But what's his motive? He had already blackmailed Aiden into giving back his truck, or at least that's my best guess. But if he kills Aiden, the blackmail stops. Unless Aiden has something on him, and he felt shutting Aiden up was worth losing whatever he gained from Aiden."

"What if he wanted to make sure Aiden didn't take the truck again. Or maybe he just did it because he's killed before and he's mean," Sophie said.

"What do you mean he killed before?" Mable sat forward and for the first time in Esther's memory her eyes were narrow, and she looked angry.

"He was in for manslaughter. He killed a man in a bar fight," Sophie said.

"Move him to the top of the list," Grandma Mable said. "He had a motive and the means, not to mention the fact he is just plain mean."

"You know who else is creepy," Sophie said. "Principal Kelly. He is totally harassing Ms. Priest and he obviously wasn't happy about his competition. Maybe he wanted Aiden gone. But could he really murder someone over a woman?"

"With a look," Nephi said. "But seriously. If he wants to hurt a kid, he just shows up out of thin air and calls their mother. However, I can't believe anyone who is such a stickler for rules would break them."

"Principal Kelly? Sophie and I heard him bend the rules by asking Ms. Priest out after Aiden died, but that's a lightweight motive. This is so frustrating." Esther stepped back to look at the wall with Mable. "We aren't even sure who the target is. It could have been Nephi."

Mable opened a diet pop. "Women are never a lightweight motive. Love is a common reason for killing."

"You're right, but with drugs? Principal Kelly?" Sophie said.

"Well, then, who had access to the drugs?" Grandma Mable said.

Esther wrote *fentanyl-cocaine.* "Mr. Green." His name was first on her list.

"Jackson and Bubba could have had access to Jackson's dad's drugs, even if they didn't know how lethal they were," Sophie said.

"Anyone with money," Mable said. "We're back to motive. What about Nevaeh? Could she have been angry enough with Aiden for leaving her mom?"

"Maybe," Esther said. "I saw some kids talk to Mr. Green the night of the Ball, so maybe he sold drugs to students, and Nevaeh could have bought drugs from him. But she doesn't seem like the murdering type."

"Ted Bundy didn't seem like a killer, but he was. Put her down," Mable said.

"Who's Ted Bundy?" Nephi asked.

"Don't look him up. You'll never sleep again." Mable looked serious. "Let's look at each person and their relationships."

"Ms. Priest was dating Aiden who had just broken up with Angelica and upset Nevaeh, Angelica's daughter," Esther said.

"How does Angelica feel about Ms. Priest? Does she blame her?" Mable sat forward.

"They seem to be good friends. She brought her coffee and soup today. If she was mad at her, it seems like that's gone now that Aiden is gone." Esther chewed her lip and closed her eyes, trying to think. "At first I thought of her, but how does she stand to gain from Aiden dying, unless it is just pure revenge."

"We're missing something. Does anyone else like Ms. Priest enough to get rid of Aiden?" Mable asked.

"Only our nerdy principal," Sophie said. "But you can't date someone you work with, right? When he asked her out, she turned him down. I guess she could make a formal complaint and he could get fired. He also comes in every day to tell her lame jokes. He shows up at the oddest moments."

"Love is a strong motive," Mable said. "Especially when someone is rejected by someone they love. He has power and prestige. Did she really turn him down?"

"We heard her turn him down. That doesn't mean he won't keep asking her or bothering her. But what does that have to do with Parker? I can't imagine who would want to hurt Parker," Esther said.

"I can," Sophie said. "Anyone who is jealous, doesn't know him, or maybe is just a lunatic involved in school violence. We can't rule out that it was a random crime by some other person at school."

"What if he was just a distraction? You know? Something you do to throw someone off?" Nephi said.

"Whoa. Way to problem solve. He's right," Sophie said. "The killer could have had Aiden as a target all along, and poisoned Parker to throw us off his scent."

"What does a killer smell like?" Nephi gave Sophie a cheesy grin.

"Back to square one." Esther put the marker on the bench. "We need to tell Papa J about the Low Tide and Mr. Green. Come on. We can't put it off any longer."

Chapter Fifteen

I Object!

"Mom! You went to a bar?" Esther's mom started pacing in the kitchen. "And you took Esther and Sophie?"

"I made them wait in the car with hot chocolate. It didn't take me too long to get the information I wanted." Mable's eyes twinkled. "It was just like the good old days when I worked with your father and the military police in the army."

Esther's mom talked with her hands. Every word was emphasized with a gesture. "I know, but seriously, Mom. I have been telling Esther this is risky and to let the police do their work and now I learn you're encouraging her?"

"Mom, I'm not a child any . . ."

"Esther James, I will thank you to stay out of this."

"But . . ."

Papa J continued eating his ice cream, only glancing at the fray once in a while. Finally, he scrapped his bowl and cleared his throat.

"What?" her mom said.

"You know I have to call Kohornen now. This is new evidence that might crack his case. You might get called in as a witness, Mable."

"Better and better! Now the whole town will know you took our kids to a bar."

"Just the parking lot."

"Mom!"

Papa J put his bowl in the sink and started washing dishes while his wife and mother-in-law practiced honest communication at the table.

"I think I'm going to go home." Sophie smiled sheepishly at Esther.

"Like a rat leaving a sinking ship. I'll text Nephi to see if he can walk you. It's dark out." When Esther picked up her phone, she found a text from Paisley that she must have missed in the chaos.

> Text from Paisley: *He is breathing on his own but still on oxygen and weak. He sends his love to everyone.*
> Text to Paisley: *I feel like crying. I am so relieved. Does this mean he will get better?*
> Text to Esther: *I did cry. We still don't know if there is any permanent damage. I am coming to school tomorrow. I have a haunted house to work on. See you in the morning. Night.*
> Text to Paisley: *See you!*

> Text to Nephi: *Can you walk Sophie home?*
> Text to Esther: *Why can't you? Just walk her to the corner.*
> Text to Nephi: *Because I am about to be yelled at by Mom, again.*
> Text from Nephi: **Smile emoji* *laugh emoji* *laugh emoji* *laugh emoji* I'll do it.*

Miss Molly's warm body was sleeping in its favorite place, on Esther's pillow, on her hair. Esther laid still, eyes closed, having moved for the fifth time, only to have Molly knead the pillow and move right back in place. *Please sleep, please sleep.* Frustration wrestled with exhaustion in her stomach. *I'm hungry. Sleep. Please.* Flashes of the day's events moved through her mind like puzzle pieces looking for a place they belonged.

She opened on eye and peeked at her bedside clock. Ten whole minutes had passed. It was 10:15. She sighed, and rolled over, moving Miss Molly to the next pillow, and then turning her pillow over, pounding on it and adjusting it. She plopped down on it and squished it again, rolled over, and . . . 10:17.

She picked up her cell. No messages, no social media anything. Everything that had happened at the ball, at the trailer park, at the candy shop moved through her mind to new places with the new information about Mr. Green's drug dealing, over and over again.

She typed Angelica Rose, Nevaeh, Fire, California, and hit search. California and fire brought up news stories about forest fires. She updated her search and filtered it to news, guesstimating approximate dates.

Her eyes grew, she sat up and turned on the light. A picture of Nevaeh and Angelica Rose standing outside a burning house, with their backs to the cameras was the first thing that popped up. The headline read, "Fatal Fire Killing Father Started by Child Playing with Matches." The article went on to say that Angelica Rose told firefighters that she was hired as a nanny to keep an eye on Nevaeh because she was a problem child and fire starting was something she did. She was being homeschooled after an incident of fire starting at school. There was another photo deeper in the article of Nevaeh's haunted face and Angelica. What interested Esther was not only Nevaeh's heartbroken face, but how different Angelica looked.

She looked like a California surfer. She was dressed in very different clothes. A tee shirt with a surf logo, big sunglasses, tight jeans, and tennis shoes. Her hair was still in a tight ponytail and totally controlled, but Esther had wondered who she was and checked the photo caption.

Esther texted Sophie: *You should see what I found.*

She sent the link to the article.

Sophie texted Esther: *Come over and let's do some research. I have an idea.*

Esther wanted to but it was a school night.

Text to Sophie: *It's late!*

Text to Esther: **Laughing emoji* I always come there. Your turn. I've got the equipment.*

Esther slipped out of her covers, took paper from her desk, and wrote a note, *"At Sophie's,"* and left it on her pillow in case anyone noticed she was gone. She put on a sweatshirt and sweats and quietly made her way down the stairs to the front door.

I'm not really sneaking out. I'm old enough to go. I'm just being qui-etly polite, so I don't wake anyone up. Miss Molly meowed and Esther realized she had been followed. Their aging dog, Lady, stood silently watching her with Molly. "Go back to bed," she whispered as she slipped out the door before Molly could follow.

Sophie just lived down the street, but in the dark and fog, it felt a lot further to Esther. The rhythmic ocean was the only sound. Her heart beat rapidly as she quietly ran along the side of the narrow gravel road.

Sophie's house was nestled in pine trees on the beachfront side of their street. The pathway through the pines had solar lights. She was almost to the door when she heard an owl. She stopped to see where it was. Then she heard it again. It wasn't an owl.

"Sophie," she hissed.

"Over here." Sophie was leaning out her bedroom window. Luckily her house was one story and wandered in odd shapes. It had a basement which was rare for the coast, making the window about shoulder height for Esther. There was a large landscaping rock under the window she used to climb up and into Sophie's dark bedroom.

"Shush," Sophie whispered. She took Esther's hand and pulled her through the shadows in her minimalist bedroom. "Take your flip flops off."

Esther left them in Sophie's room, and they padded down the hallway to a room with a keypad at the end. Sophie punched in the numbers and used her thumbprint to open the lock. They passed onto the top of a stairway in the dark.

The auto lights came on and the girls took the stairs down to another metal door. Past the metal door, they entered her parent's lab. The lights came on when they opened the door. The space was white, sterile, and the single window was solid white plexiglass. Air scrub-bers, filters, and dehumidifiers ran quietly. They passed a large bank of computers and equipment. Sophie led the familiar way through the room that looked like a college chem lab. Just beyond that was a gated play area from Sophie's childhood and then, behind a wall of safety glass was Sophie's personal den.

The wall had a massive screen for her projector which she used for television or video games. A sleek black sit-and-stand desk had computers, screens, and game controllers. Her chair was a yoga ball. Esther pulled up a bean bag while Sophie sat at her laptop.

"After I read the news article, I had an idea," Sophie said.

"Shouldn't we whisper?" Esther asked.

Sophie shook her head, "The room is soundproof. Dad designed it that way for the days he plays videogames." She smiled. "I thought we should check to see if we can find a wedding announcement for Angelica's last marriage and then look at her social media and the social media of the husband she lost."

"Genius."

"Yes, I am." Sophie rapidly typed in the search. Hundreds of answers popped up. She narrowed the search and projected her screen on the wall.

Esther's mouth fell open. "Oh, my cranberry sauce." She stood up and stepped closer as if it would change what she was seeing.

"E. I'm rubbing off on you. You're food swearing," Sophie giggled.

The wall top to bottom with wedding announcements. They were all for Angelica Rose. "These can't be all her," Esther said.

"There are probably many women with the same name. Let's open them," Sophie said.

One by one they opened the announcements. When their sorting was finished, they had four wedding announcements. They all had photos of Angelica Rose.

"Are you seeing what I see? She doesn't look the same in a single photo." Esther stepped back to look at all four at once. In one of the three photos, she had blonde hair with dark roots, in one her black hair was short and spikey and her makeup was distracting, and in the last one, she looked like herself. Esther was fascinated by the photo that looked like it was the first, the oldest, and where she was the youngest. In the picture she was almost frowning. She was pregnant, and the man looked twenty years older than she was. It was a news story from the society pages of a New York newspaper. The title read, "20-year-old hooks ARTINTel Company founder with a Fake Pregnancy."

"Let's look up the husbands," Esther said.

"Crepes, check the time. It's midnight," Sophie said. "We better get to bed for school."

Esther stretched and yawned. "Okay. But what do we have here? It looks like she has been married at least four times. Each man seemed to be someone important or successful. And each man is dead. Some from natural causes and one from fire and one from a hit and run driver. It looks like they all loved her at one time."

Sophie yawned. "But that doesn't explain why she ended up with Nevaeh's father and why they weren't married, or why she adopted Nevaeh."

"I don't know, but I need some sleep."

"Me too." Sophie shut down the computer and led Esther back upstairs. She peeked out the door, and they slipped out in the dark.

Esther stepped out of the front door, turned and whispered, "We'll pick you up in the morning. Let's sleep on this."

"Night, E."

"Night."

Chapter Sixteen

The Subcommittee

Nephi and Esther picked up Sophie on the way to school. It was another gray, Oregon Coast day. The old truck blew through clouds of fog. They took the extra one block loop silently, checking the ocean. It was something he did on the regular to watch the incoming weather. Esther loved the glimpse of the beach. The ocean was winter angry and washing in closer to shore. A massive log rolled in the surf waiting for a wave to push it onto the sand. On the distant horizon, a small line of pale blue separated the green, gray water from the rain clouds. To the north, the clouds released a sheet of rain miles offshore and heading their way.

"The sun's going to come out today," Nephi said and continued to drive toward school.

Sophie leaned over the seat. "I never did ask how things ended up last night? Are you grounded?"

Esther turned in her seat and faced Sophie. "I have no idea. They talked about making me do a disgusting chore. Mom was mad enough at Grandma that maybe they'll forget about us. They were still talking when I went to bed. Luckily, Mom was out on a call for work when I got up."

"Phew. Maybe she'll forget about it by the time you see her again."

Nephi laughed, "Not likely. I love seeing goody, goody Esther get into trouble."

"Is that so you don't feel so lonely when you get in trouble every day?" Sophie said.

"Hey now." Nephi stopped talking.

"I did one more check this morning. Guess what I found?" Sophie said.

"Give."

"An engagement announcement for Nevaeh's dad and Angelica Rose." Sophie grinned and wiggled her brows. "Say it. I'm a genius. Say it."

Esther laughed. "You're a genius like me. But why adopt Nevaeh? Still, after last night I am pretty sure Nevaeh isn't the problem. I'm sure it has something to do with money."

"That doesn't rule out Jackson or Bubba from getting the drugs from his dad and bringing them to the ball," Esther shrugged. "We need to let Papa J or Kohornen know her history."

"What about Nevaeh? If she is as dangerous as we think, we should talk to your mom. Let's talk to your parents after school," Sophie said.

Nephi pulled into the school parking lot. "Look. The BMW. I wonder if Paisley drove it."

"She texted and told me she was coming today." Esther gathered her things while he parked.

"Why didn't you tell me." He raised his arm and smelled his shirt.

"Did you just smell your underarm? Good thing I'm always ready to take a picture," Sophie said, pointing her phone at Nephi. "This one is going out on every platform I have."

"Sophie!"

Laughing, Sophie waved her phone, jumped out of the car, and ran for the library doors. She was inside before Nephi made it halfway across the parking lot.

Carrying Sophie's backpack, Esther waved at Nephi as she climbed the library steps. She pulled the door open and breathed in the scent of books before she realized they still had a lot of cleaning up to do. Her shoulders drooped.

"We should have slept more. There's a ton of work to do," Esther said.

Sophie was standing by the door looking as stunned as she felt. "I almost forgot how bad it was."

"Are you really going to post that?"

"I didn't get a picture. Pinky swear."

"Let me see." She held out her hand until Sophie relinquished her phone. Esther typed in Sophie's pin and opened her photos. "You did take his picture, just not smelling his armpit. Nice picture. She swiped and there was another picture of him from right after they got in the car. Then four or five photos from the parking lot at the Low Tide. Swipe. More pictures. "Sophie? I think you like him."

"Give me that phone."

Esther held it up so Sophie couldn't reach it. "I think you like my uncle."

"Give it." Sophie jumped. Esther laughed.

The door opened and a very thin Paisley walked into the middle of Esther's game of keep away. "Hi. I'm back. What's on the phone?"

Esther, Paisley, and Sophie sat close to the library fireplace. The flame warmed Esther's hands.

"Parker has his phone now," Paisley said. "But he was still asleep when I left. Mom and Dad haven't left his side."

"What do you think?" Esther asked. "Will he be okay, or will there be damage to his lungs?"

"I am more worried about his mind and oxygen deprivation. If he weren't always working out and running, I think it would be a different story. I'm hoping all the time he spent sweating with Nephi will help him heal faster." She smiled weakly. "I never thought I would be happy to have them smelling up the house. I will never complain again."

"I will," Sophie smiled. "What are friends for? I can't wait until he gets back. I have a whole new list of nicknames and jokes. I'm working on a Snow White dad joke involving a poisoned apple. Maybe I'll sell tickets for wake-up kisses. Too soon?"

"Sophie!" Paisley laughed. "I missed you."

"What's that?" Esther walked to the west doors. Red and blue lights on the top of a squad car in the parking caught her attention. "It's Neilson and Kohornen." They'd parked just outside the doors in a no-parking zone.

"What are they here for?" Sophie rushed to the doors with Paisley, standing on her tiptoes to see better. "I wonder if they're looking for

Green's tow truck. He always parks in the lot. Maybe they will search it for drugs."

"For drugs? What did I miss?" Paisley asked.

Sophie smiled. "A lot. After we learned what was in Parker's system, we decided to find out who had access to it or sold it on the street. We asked River Peace. He told us drugs like fentanyl and cocaine were sold at low tide. We thought he was crazy, but Mable figured it out. Low Tide is that dive bar on the south end of town. We went there with Mable, and she found out Mr. Green will sell you drugs if you call for a tow."

"Wait. What? You went to a bar?" Paisley tilted her head, drew her chin in, and looked a lot like Esther's mother.

"Not inside," Esther said. "We waited outside. Grandma Mable went in. She's brilliant."

"Oh, that's okay then. Seriously. Your grandma rocks."

The squad car doors opened. "They're coming inside. I guess they aren't waiting for Mr. Green." Esther stepped to the side and motioned Sophie and Paisley away from the window, Kohornen and Neilson passed by the west doors and entered the school through the main hall.

"What are they doing here?" Esther said.

The girls quickly jogged to the doors that joined the library to the inner hallway. Kohornen and Neilson passed the doors and rounded the corner in the direction of the principal's office.

All three girls walked softly to the corner and peeked around it in time to see them disappear into the main office.

"I hope Bridget is working in the office and listens in," Esther whispered.

"I'll text her." Paisley took out her phone. "Let's go back to the library. I know I should go to class, but I'm so exhausted. I'll go next period."

Esther's phone chimed. Her head spun to see if there was a teacher nearby. "The last thing I need is my cell confiscated. Let's go back." She turned around to go back to the library.

"Crepes," Sophie hissed. Simon, the janitor was pushing a cart straight at them. They rushed to the library.

The library doors swung shut. Esther stood off to the side and looked out the window. The janitor stood outside the door looking right at her, with no expression. A full minute passed before he turned and pushed his cart with one squeaky wheel in the direction of the office.

"Do you think he'll tell someone we're out of class?" Paisley said.

"What's going on?" Ms. Priest asked.

Startled, Esther realized she was standing right behind her. "Sorry. Kohornen and Neilson, your dad, are here. We had to see where they went. They're in the principal's office."

"Exactly where they belong," Sophie smirked. "Did your dad spend his youth waiting outside the principal's office?"

Ms. Priest broke into a smile. "My dad? I'll never tell. Paisley, shouldn't you be in class?"

Before Paisley answered, her cell phone vibrated. She read the text. "They're bringing Nevaeh to the office."

"Nevaeh?" Esther said.

Paisley's phone buzzed again.

Ms. Priest folded her arms. "Silence your phone. Don't make me confiscate it."

Paisley's phone vibrated again. "Now Bridget says they have a search warrant. The school secretary is giving them access to Nevaeh's school email and online work. She had to give Neilson her locker code. He's going to search it. Bridget is going to her class to ask her to go to Principal Kelly's office."

"No. I can't believe they think she is a suspect," Esther said. "I need to go call Parker."

"Can they question her without her mother?" Sophie asked.

"Good question," Ms. Priest said. "I am not going to confiscate your phones. You are going to put them away and I am going to the teacher's lounge via the office for a cup of tea. I didn't see you, and we didn't have this conversation. And girls—do not get yourself or me into trouble. Just because you like someone doesn't mean they didn't do something wrong. People make mistakes all the time. Let the officers do their job. We have a messy library to clean up."

"But . . ." Esther said.

Ms. Priest held a hand up. "I am leaving before Principal Kelly shows up and confiscates your phones. I suggest you put them away." Ms. Priest left the library.

"She's right." Sophie looked around the room. "This place is a disaster, and we do think everyone we like is innocent. We like Jackson's art, so he's innocent. We like Nevaeh, so she couldn't be a killer."

"Do you really think she could do it?" Paisley asked.

"Actually, we think the most likely person is Nevaeh's mother," Sophie said. "And everyone thought Ted Bundy was a nice guy. He admitted to killing multiple victims in four years before he was executed. No one knows how many victims he had."

Paisley shook her head and chuckled. "How do you know these things, Sophie?"

Esther frowned and looked at the west doors. "Wait. Do you hear sirens?"

"I hear them," Paisley said. They stood, quietly listening.

Suddenly, Bridget came into the library like a storm cloud.

"They are such jerks! They made me go get Nevaeh like she had a phone call and I had to lead her to her doom." Bridget wiped a tear running mascara down her cheek with her sleeve.

The west doors opened, and Angelica Rose came in with a tray of cookies. "Hello girls. How is Ms. Priest? I thought she could use some chocolate, as in chocolate chips."

"I guess this is the place to be." Sophie graciously took the plate of cookies and put them on the counter. Paisley reached out for one and Sophie slapped her hand, without losing her cheesy grin.

"The police are with Nevaeh in the principal's office," Bridget said, before sniffing loudly. She looked down at her shaking hands. She folded her arms and put her chin up.

"I'm sure everything is fine." Angelica Rose gave a knowing smile and winked. She began cleaning up the remnants of the party still strewn throughout the room.

Esther gave Sophie a look, eyes wide, brows up. Sophie's mouth fell open, and she mouthed holy crepes in Esther's direction.

Sirens. Loud and close. The girls ran to the west doors. An ambulance pulled up in front of the squad car and medics jumped out with their boxes and a gurney and ran through the main hall toward the office.

"Ms. Rose?" Bridget said.

"What's all that noise." She smiled and put the stack of books she was carrying on a table.

"It's an ambulance. They went to the office." Bridget pointed in the direction of the office. "You know. Where your daughter is."

"Oh. Oh, my." Angelica left briskly through the door that led toward the office.

Ms. Priest opened the library door. "You girls stay here. I'm going to the office to see what's happening and make sure we're all safe."

Medics came back around the corner and down the hall running and pushing a gurney with Nevaeh strapped to it. One of them held an IV bag in the air. Ms. Priest ran to the gurney and held Nevaeh's hand. They took the ramp and loaded her with Ms. Priest and left, with their lights and sirens clearing the road. Angelica walked past the inside library door.

Sophie opened the west door, and they all stood on the stairs watching Angelica walk calmly across the parking lot. She gave the girls a funny look, waved, and got in her car. She drove out of the parking lot in the same direction as the ambulance.

"What if Nevaeh's mother poisoned her? Why did they suspect Nevaeh?" Esther said. "I can't believe it. They know Green is selling the drugs. What do they know that we don't?"

"Her motive." Sophie bit her bottom lip. "I know you like her, E. But she was seriously hurt by Aiden. What if they think she poisoned the candy to get back at him for hurting Ms. Rose? Her life has kind of been one long train wreck. What if all the loss has made her a little crazier than we thought?"

Esther's shoulder's slumped and she let out a long breath. "I guess it's possible. She just doesn't seem like . . . I know, I know. Serial killers are nice neighbors." The wind blew strands of Esther's hair into her face. She tucked them behind her ear.

"Well, I don't believe it," Bridget said. "And what is wrong with her mother? Can you imagine what my mother would be doing if you told her I was in the office with the police?"

"Your mom? Madison Merriweather?" Paisley said. "She would have flown into that office and torn the principal limb from limb. She's so protective, she makes a mother bear look like a kitten. She's like a . . . a . . . mother monster!"

"Mine too," Esther said.

Sophie put her hands on her hips. "Last night E and I did some online research. Nevaeh's mom has been married and widowed multiple times."

"What we can't figure out is why kill Aiden?" Esther said. "She probably inherited money when her husbands died but killing Aiden wouldn't get her anything. They weren't married, which is why we can't totally rule out Nevaeh and revenge."

"But the way her mom acted was so bizarre," Bridget said.

"Could she be in shock?" Paisley asked.

"If she was, she was the calmest person in shock I've ever seen," Bridget said.

"How many have you seen?" Esther asked.

"You've met my mother. I've seen her leave a wave of shock behind her when she thinks something is wrong or someone harmed me."

"More importantly," Esther said. "What is wrong with Nevaeh?"

"Think about the symptoms," Sophie said. "It must be the same poison?"

Paisley pulled her key fob out of her pocket. "We need to get up to the hospital and see if she's okay. I'll drive."

Before the girls made it to Paisley's car, the main doors opened, and Officer Neilson came out with Jackson in handcuffs.

Esther's mouth fell open. "Why are they taking Jackson in? We have to stop them. They don't know about Angelica's past."

Korhonen drove slowly out of the parking lot and they watched as he headed to the police station.

"Didn't Papa J tell them that Jackson's dad was the one who was selling drugs? Why does everyone keep assuming it must be Jackson?" Esther closed her eyes and put her hands over her face. "Of course they blame him. He has a motive because of the fight and social media post, and we just proved that he has access to the drugs that killed Aiden. How could we be so stupid?"

"You didn't do this," Bridget said.

Sophie took off her glasses and began gesturing wildly with them while she spoke. "Will anyone ever give Jackson a break? He is a great artist and takes care of his father like his father should be taking care of him!"

"It gets better and better," Paisley said. "Look."

Mr. Green pulled into the lot and parked his tow truck in his usual spot, the middle of town, where students have car trouble and he's close to anyone calling for a tow.

"I wonder if he sells drugs to kids?" Bridget asked.

Esther spun on her heels, eyes wide. "Why wouldn't he? I saw kids at the truck the night of the dance. He obviously knows his drugs killed Mr. Van Doren. Even if he didn't poison the candy, he knows who bought the drugs from him! That . . . That . . .!"

Something snapped. Something that had been planted deep in Esther when she was a child began dumping adrenaline into her system. *Hold on. Hold. Don't lose it. He helped poison Parker!* An idea grew into a plan. It would require her to bend the truth, but it had to be done.

Esther balled her hands into fists. She pressed her lips together and began marching to Mr. Green's truck.

"Esther, stop!" Paisley grabbed her arm, but she yanked it free.

"Don't stop her," Sophie said. She caught up to Esther.

Mr. Green was slouched in his seat, texting someone. Esther knocked on the driver's door. She smiled at Mr. Green with her lips, but her eyes were narrowed.

He sat up and looked at her, his whiskery face and baseball hat hid his feelings. The power window rolled down slowly while Esther waited, every muscle in her body tense, her jaw clenched.

She tipped her head and gave him the smug kind of smile a teacher gives a student she has just caught passing notes in class. "Mr. Green?"

He was silent.

"The police think Jackson used drugs he got from you to kill Mr. Van Doren. They just took him to the station."

He pulled his hat off, slack jawed and wide eyed, he said, "What?"

She knew she was taking a calculated risk. She was relying on Green having any kind of love for his son.

"When?" Mr. Green said and started the truck's motor.

"It isn't too late," Esther said. "They left with him in handcuffs just before you pulled into the parking lot. If you hurry, you can catch up to them and tell them the truth."

Sophie held up her fist. Esther put her arm out, like a mother trying to stop a running child, but it was no use. She pulled Esther's arm down and standing on her toes so she could see him, barked, "You did this to him! You sold the drugs the killer used to poison everyone at the dance. Jackson's wonderful and you're going to let him take the fall for killing Aiden with the drugs you sell! Are you going to let Jackson pay the price?"

Esther touched Sophie's shoulder, interrupting her. "Sophie's right. I believe you love Jackson. If you go now, it's not too late to make this right. But before you go. Who bought drugs from you? Was it Angelica Rose?"

Mr. Green blinked. And then Esther watched understanding cross his wrinkled face as the color rose from his neck and through his beard.

"They took Jackson to jail?"

"He left in handcuffs in a squad car. They're treating him like an adult. He's over eighteen."

Mr. Green's eyes closed. Cringing, he rubbed his face and beard with both hands and then ran them through his wild hair.

"Get out of my way." Mr. Green looked at them and through gritted teeth said, "I may have done a lot of bad things, but I love my boy. I love my boy." He rolled the window up while he gunned the truck's motor.

Esther and Sophie jumped back, giving him room to back up and roar out of the parking lot.

Realizing she was holding her breath, Esther loudly exhaled. "Sorry, Sophie."

"I'm glad you held me back. I wanted to climb up there and shave his face with my fingernails." Sophie gave her a friendly push.

Mouths open, shocked, Bridget and Paisley were still standing by Paisley's car. Esther took another deep breath, trying to slow down her heart, and walked back to them. "We need to be very careful. I have an idea, but I'm not sure. When Ms. Priest just lectured us, I remembered something. If I'm right, Nevaeh is in serious danger."

Bridget laughed so loud she quickly covered her mouth. "Sorry! I thought you were going to get us all killed. I think I'm going to throw up."

Sophie slapped her on the back. "I would have taken him out for you."

"Good grief . . ." Esther chuckled and climbed in the front seat of Paisley's car.

"Where to?" Paisley asked.

Esther realized Paisley was asking her. "We need to think this through. We're missing something." She closed her eyes and rubbed them and took another deep breath and blew it out slowly. Her hands shook. "I can't think."

"No matter what he does, shouldn't we try to tell the hospital that we think Nevaeh may be affected by the same drug?" Sophie asked.

Esther turned around in her seat and looked back at Sophie. "I agree, but what if we went to the police station first? Do you think they would let me talk to Jackson? I want to try. He kept the books for his dad. He knows who called his dad for a special tow." She made air quotes, when she said *tow*.

Paisley started the car. "Okay. But Sophie's sticking by me. She is a fierce nerd, and I need her around to protect me while you're at the station."

Bridget laughed again. "I'm sorry. I don't know what's wrong with me."

Chapter Seventeen

Behind the Mask

In the short drive to the police station, the rain picked up. The car's windshield wipers ran at a furious pace, but it was still hard to see.

Covering her eyes with her hands, Esther tried to remember everything that happened at the ball, and what they observed after it was over. "We have the answers. I know it. We just have to put all the pieces of the puzzle together."

"I wish we had Grandma Mable and her murder wall," Sophie said.

"We don't. And if we go home now, we won't be allowed to leave." Esther pushed up her sleeves. "I keep having this flash, a memory from the ball."

She turned in her seat so she could see Sophie. "Where were you right before it happened?"

Sophie closed her eyes and was silent for a moment. "I remember it all. When we arrived, we all met by the fireplace. Paisley, Bridget, Nephi, Parker, and you."

"That's right," Bridget said. "I had just arrived with my mom, and I was embarrassed to be there without a date. But Paisley asked me to dance with her and Nephi."

"You were embarrassed? Me too! I told Esther and Parker I would hold up the wall." Sophie smiled at Bridget.

Esther looked intently over the back seat at Sophie. "That's when Parker said he was hungry, so Sophie and I went with him to the refreshment table. Remember?"

Sophie bit her lip and squinted her eyes. "We know the poison was in some of the apples, but we don't know how many."

Esther sat up straight and said, "I know who it was and I know why!"

"Who?" Paisley looked at her, and Esther grabbed the wheel, pulling them back into their lane.

"I don't know how to prove it, though." Esther watched Paisley driving, but she was back at the ball, remembering. "Right when we got to the refreshment table, Ms. Rose brought out a tray of apples with what looked like diamonds on them. Ms. Priest was impressed and asked about them. After explaining that the diamonds were rock candy, she made a point of giving one to Ms. Priest and inviting her to try it. She looked annoyed when Ms. Priest said she would eat it after making the root beer. I thought she was annoyed about Nevaeh's costume."

"Who?" Paisley said.

Esther said, "Eyes on the road."

"E! Why did she do it!" Sophie leaned closer to the front seat.

"Well, think about it. They were asking kids not to eat candy until we were ready. Remember who ate it anyway?"

"Jackson and Bubba. I was so irritated I took an apple away from Bubba and threw it away."

"I think you may have saved his life. You kept him from finishing it. That's why he only got a little sick." Esther shook her head. The girls moved in closer.

"Do you remember what happened next? I'll never forget it," Esther said.

"Aiden asked if it was time to let everyone eat right after I threw away Bubba's candy?" Sophie tipped her head and thought.

"Yes. And then Parker asked me to dance. I can't believe I didn't see it sooner. I was distracted. Every time I tried to remember, I would feel so bad about missing my last chance to dance with Parker, and I focused on my mistake. I missed the obvious things that happened at the same time."

"Wait! You're right. I think I understand." Sophie smacked the back of Paisley's seat. "Why didn't we think of this before?"

"What?" Bridget asked. "Will someone please tell me who did it, please?"

Esther looked at Sophie. "Ms. Rose handed Ms. Priest an apple from the furthest corner of her tray, which was odd. The poison was meant for Ms. Priest, but she gave her apple to Aiden."

"See?" Sophie said. "Angelica was upset because she lost Mr. Van Doren to Ms. Priest. Nevaeh said they were running out of money. Angelica had done a lot of work already to bag Aiden and his money."

Esther nodded and finished Sophie's thought. "Aiden had money, and she tried to kill Ms. Priest to get her out of the way. She's a widow four times over. We think she killed her four husbands for their money? Then why not Ms. Priest?"

Paisley's eyes grew. Her mouth dropped open. "You think she's a black widow? A serial killer?"

"But how could she get away with four murders?" Bridget asked.

Esther's hands were shaking again. She closed them into a fist. "She must be smart. They were all written off as accidents. I don't know how. My guess is this time, she thought she could make it look like Jackson and Bubba did it. They were the perfect people to blame it on. Everyone knew about the threats. No one would care about them or stand up for two bullies."

"But wait," Sophie said. "How do we tie her to the drugs? We've got no proof she did it. We were all around the candy, even Nevaeh. And Nevaeh is the one that is sick. What if Nevaeh did it to help her mom and was exposed to the drugs?"

Esther shook her head. "I know we should look at motive and facts, but do you honestly think Nevaeh would do that? Think about the strange way Ms. Rose followed Nevaeh to the hospital."

Bridget said, "Maybe she wants Nevaeh out of the way. What if she is really a cold, hard killer and done with Nevaeh because her money is almost gone? Maybe she thinks Nevaeh is keeping her from getting a new man? I've heard some of my mom's friends complain about dating with kids."

"Why would Nevaeh interfere with her finding someone?" Esther asked.

"I always worry that I am the reason my mom doesn't date. And I have read in *Today's Teen Magazine* that it is hard to blend families."

Esther chuckled. "Well, we know that's accurate research. I guess it makes sense. But haven't you noticed how pale and sick Nevaeh has been lately. It can't be a onetime dose. What if her money isn't really gone? What if Angelica is lying to her? Think about how valuable her business is. What if Angelica inherits if Nevaeh dies?"

"We should have followed the money," Sophie said.

Esther bit her lip. "I think it's something far worse. I think she is going to try to pin everything on Nevaeh to protect herself. I bet she has a suicide note in Nevaeh's bedroom or backpack. All she has to do is write a note on Nevaeh's laptop that says she killed Aiden because he left them for Ms. Priest. She could even gaslight her and make it look like she lit the fire that killed her father, or worse. Nevaeh probably has enough drugs in her system to look like an addict who poisoned people for revenge and then killed herself."

Paisley pulled into the station parking lot and turned off the car. "I hate to say it, but I think you're right. One carefully penned suicide note could be enough to take suspicion off Ms. Rose."

Esther took off her seatbelt. "I think you're right. That's why we're here. One person can help us prove she did it . . ." Esther chewed on her bottom lip.

"Are we here to get Papa J?" Sophie said.

Esther shook her head, no. "Him." She pointed at the door to the station. Jackson Green was standing in the pouring rain, head down, hands in his pockets, all alone.

Esther opened her car door and got out, letting the rain wet her hair and wash her face. "Jackson!"

His head snapped up, and his brows drew together. "What are you doing here?"

"We know you didn't do it. We want your help."

He rolled his eyes. "I have real-life problems to take care of. I don't have time for a couple of amateur detectives."

"Nevaeh is in the hospital. We're afraid her mother won't tell them what's happening or what she has in her system. We think her mother is the person who killed Aiden and is trying to kill Nevaeh with the same drugs. We think you can help her," Esther shouted over the rain.

"What?" He tilted his head and studied her drenched face. "What do you want from me?"

Pointing at the doors to the station, Esther said, "First, what happened in there?"

Jackson closed his eyes and clenched his jaw. When he opened them and looked down at her, anger rolled across his face.

"Jackson! Please."

He looked back down and cleared his throat. She waited, shivering in the cold.

Jackson looked Esther in the eyes. "My dad took the fall for me. He came in yelling that I was innocent and that he poisoned Aiden Van Doren."

"But he didn't . . ." She shook her head and said, "Are you sure he confessed? Do they believe him?"

Jackson rolled his eyes and pushed his hands deeper into his pockets. "Trust me. He confessed and they believe him."

"But wait." She reached out and touched his arm. He yanked it away. "No, wait, Jackson, I think you can prove Angelica did it. You kept your dad's books, right?"

He didn't move.

"Did he ever tow Angelica Rose?"

Jackson looked up, blinking. "He . . . yes . . . I thought it was strange. He towed her four times, and she has a brand-new car."

"I knew it! Do you have a record of all the times he towed her? Jackson nodded. "I do. But . . . I mean. Are you saying she bought the drugs that killed Aiden from my dad? That means I have to get my own dad in trouble. Why would she kill Aiden, her own daughter? I have to go back in there and tell the detective to let my dad go!"

"No! You have to help." Esther touched his arm again and looked directly into his eyes. "If we don't go up and tell the doctors what's wrong, I'm afraid Nevaeh might die. They took her away in an ambulance right before they took you. The hospital could leave her alone with Angelica."

He turned, thinking. "We can't let her die."

"I know. You have to come help us. We're going to the hospital. Then we're going to get your books and come back here." Esther pulled him in the direction of the car. "Come on! We can't waste any more time."

Sophie stood beside the car, holding the passenger door open. He got in the back.

"Move over, big guy. Make room," Sophie said as she slid into the back seat with Jackson.

The emergency room doors were locked. There was a buzzer with a sign that said press for admittance. Esther pushed the button once, twice, and then danced on it until a voice came over the speaker.

"Stop! Can I help you?" A voice with a strong southern accent asked.

Esther looked into the camera on the ceiling. "We know what's wrong with Nevaeh! She's been affected by a drug. It's an overdose. We need to talk to the doctor," Esther barked at the speaker. No one responded. Then ,after a buzzing sound, the double doors swung open, and they ran to the waiting room.

Ms. Priest stood up when everyone barreled into the empty room. "You're soaked."

"Ms. Priest." Esther pointed at the glass door that led into the exam rooms. "Who's with Nevaeh? We know what's wrong with her. We need to talk to the doctor."

"Her mother is. Since I am not family, I have to wait out here. They won't talk to you about a patient. It breaks the rules of confidentiality."

Sophie began pounding on the glass door.

"What is going on?" A male nurse, followed by a man in a white coat and stethoscope, came into the waiting room. Angelica Rose stood behind the door.

"We know what's wrong with Nevaeh. She has fentanyl and cocaine in her system! It's an overdose." Esther's words tumbled out.

The door slammed open, and Ms. Rose shouted, "Get her out of here!"

"She did it." Jackson's deep voice barked as he pointed at Angelica.

Angelica came through the glass doors, nostrils flared, her hands balled in fists. She looked up at Jackson and changing her mind, yelled in Esther's face. "Get them out of here!"

"I can handle this . . ." The nurse started to say.

Sophie stepped between Angelica and Esther. "You're a murderer!"

Esther pulled Sophie back and Jackson held onto her angry frame. Esther was shaking, something welled up inside her, but she heard her mother's voice in her head telling her to breathe and not get angry.

Fueled by adrenalin, Esther felt eerily composed. She leaned toward Angelica Rose and said calmly, "We have proof that you tried to poison Ms. Priest, and Aiden was killed by accident. You put fentanyl and cocaine on your rock candy caramel apples and Ms. Priest gave hers to Aiden while Parker ate his before any other kids were served. We have proof that you poisoned multiple apples with fentanyl and cocaine to make it look like Jackson and Bubba did it to kill students. But we know. Mr. Green confessed to selling the drugs used for murdering Aiden. We're going to turn over all his records of anyone he has sold drugs too and you're on them for four tows. And now you're poisoning Nevaeh to make it look like an accidental overdose or suicide. Like she has remorse for murdering Aiden. And so you can inherit everything she has. But your plan didn't work. You're going to jail."

Angelica snarled at Esther, quietly. "Green can't prove a thing. I paid in cash for anything I ever bought from him." She stepped back, pointed at Esther and barked, "Get her out of here."

An announcement sounded throughout the hospital speaker. "Code gray, code gray, code gray. Emergency waiting room."

Esther turned her attention to the doctor, who stood in the doorway, gaping at the scene as it unfolded. "She's trying to kill Nevaeh, Doctor. She's been poisoning her with the same drugs that killed Aiden Van Doren. It's an overdose. Do something!"

Angelica Rose growled like a wild animal, taking Esther by the neck, but all of Esther's mother's self-defense lessons paid off. She put her hands up between Angelica's arms and pressed down hard with her elbows until Angelica had to let go while Esther stomped on her foot with her heel.

And then Jackson let go of Sophie and she took Angelica down.

"I got video!" Paisley shouted.

"Oh? I am streaming live," Bridget grinned smugly.

Sophie had her foot squarely on Angelica's back and one of her arms twisted behind her, when Jackson picked Sophie up like a child so two hospital security guards could get to Angelica and do their job.

Bridget turned her cell to her face and said, "This is Bridget reporting from the Necanicum emergency waiting room where Nevaeh Rose's mother, Angelica, has just confessed to poisoning the candy that killed Aiden Van Doren."

"You little . . . You've got nothing! Nothing, I tell you!" She flailed wildly between the security guards dragging her towards the door.

Paisley pulled a taser out of her purse.

"Uh. Ma'am. Ma'am! Put the weapon away," the larger guard demanded.

Paisley shrugged and put it away, smiling sheepishly.

Esther realized she was hearing sirens in the distance and getting closer. In less than a minute, Papa J's best friend, Officer Ironpot, entered the waiting room. The security guards held Angelica in the hallway while Ironpot cuffed her. The girls stepped out to watch Angelica as she struggled.

"What are you girls doing here?" Ironpot asked.

Sophie said, "We're streaming live! Do you have anything to say to the people?"

"Don't bother calling Sophie and Esther, because they are grounded!'" he yelled and then laughed loudly as he dragged Ms. Rose, kicking and screaming, out of the hospital doors.

Bridget ended the video and raised both hands in the air and screamed with joy. Sophie and Paisley gave each other a high five, while Esther just tried to breathe.

Ms. Priest, who had retreated to the corner of the room, closed her mouth, shook her head, and said, "Esther, Sophie, Paisley, Bridget, you're some fierce women. I am glad you're my friends and not coming for me."

"That was awesome." Jackson grinned at Sophie.

The doctor hadn't moved. Frozen, eyes wide, he finally seemed to come to. "I have to see to my patient. What drug did you say you think she's been given?

Sophie said, "Fentanyl and cocaine."

"What's going on?"

Esther spun around at the sound of Parker's voice. He stood in the doorway, holding onto the doorjamb for support. His parents were behind him. "Esther?"

"Parker!" Esther threw herself into his arms and started to shake all over. She felt him stagger, so she turned and put his arm around her shoulder for support. "You should be in bed."

He smiled weakly.

She laughed, then she cried, smiling.

Chapter Eighteen

The After Party

Parker had been moved out of intensive care before the emergency room wrestling match. The doctor in the Medical-Surgical Unit allowed family and a few friends to visit Parker in the family waiting room.

Parker leaned on Esther during the walk back to his room. Sophie and Bridget passed the nurse's station, heads down, afraid they would be asked to leave.

When they all crowded into the room, Mr. and Mrs. Stuart, smiling, moved to the doorway.

"I'm sorry," Mrs. Stuart said to Parker's nurse. "Mr. Stuart and I told Ms. Priest we would take her home. We'll take a break, so the room isn't crowded." She kissed Sophie's cheek, hugged her son, and motioned for Parker's father to follow her out.

The nurse put a blood pressure cuff on Parker's arm and pumped it up to take his blood pressure. "Are these ladies the reason we had a code gray?"

Esther grimaced and looked down. "Maybe?"

"Well, if you are, I want to shake your hand. News travels fast in Necanicum. My daughter texted me the link to your live report, Bridget. We are now officially fans. You should both be detectives when you grow up. Smart. Yes, you are."

"Can I come in?" Nephi stood at the door with three boxes of tacos from a local fast-food restaurant. "I thought Parker might be hungry, but I guess I missed everything."

"You're a mind reader. But where is everyone else's?" Sophie grabbed a taco and tots. "Where is the diet soda pop?"

"Diet?" Nephi raised his eyebrows. "Really?"

Sophie answered with a mouth full of tatter tots, "A girl has to watch her figure."

Esther chuckled while she pulled the blanket over Parker. The room was filled with flowers and cards from his family and the entire long-distance track team, as well as a group card and photo from the Oceanside High Cheer Squad.

"Esther?" Parker took her hand. "Are you okay? It sounded like it was awful. Your neck has scratches on it."

She smiled and felt her neck. "It's a little tender, I guess."

"Yes, but how are you?" He studied her face.

She smiled. "I am stronger than I thought I was. I've always avoided being triggered. I hated even being seen on social media after I was bullied for my dad going to prison. I'd rather be invisible."

"I know. That's why I'm worried. It must have been hard to confront her." Parker took her other hand.

Esther thought for a moment. "I just learned something new. Thanks to you, Paisley, Nephi, and Sophie, even Bridget. I am surrounded by friends and feel safer with you than when I was hiding in the library. Being invisible may have been safe, but I was kind of lonely."

"And now?" he asked.

"I've taken more risks than ever before in my life. I would risk anything for every person in this room. I'm happier than I have ever been. I'm sorry for the way I behaved before the dance. I'm done being afraid. I'm leaning into trust."

"Do you love me?" he asked as he broke into a smile that created a dimple in his right cheek. His eyes twinkled.

She grinned and looked at their hands. "Yes."

"Ditto."

"Ditto? Ditto?" Sophie stepped up to the bedside with her hands on her hips.

Parker laughed. "I love her. All right?"

"You better. Now, who's going for something to drink? Is the cafeteria open?"

Chapter Nineteen

Zombie with Two Left Feet

Clouds covered the moon. Twinkle lights and a few spotlights penetrated the dark night, outlining the old cannery the boosters had turned into a haunted house. To get to the cannery, families would have to cross a narrow bridge with handrails and nets for safety. The massive structure was built over the river on Pier Seven in the 1800s. It still stood strong, even though it hadn't been used in Esther's lifetime. She could hear sea lions barking and the water lapping underneath the dock.

"Jackson, this is unbelievable," Sophie said. "And sort of cute."

They were in front of the door to the cannery, but it looked exactly like the door to a medieval castle.

"How did you know how to do this? It looks so real. How long did this take?" Esther asked.

Jackson shrugged. "We planned it before everything went crazy. Someone else took the drawings and put up the plywood. It could be better, but we only had a few days to paint and decorate."

"Are you kidding me? Seriously. I feel like if I touched the stones, they would be cold and rounded. Everything looks so real." Esther reached out and touched the painted ironwork on the wooden door.

"It's just plywood walls." Jackson cleared his throat and looked down at his feet.

Sophie playfully punched his shoulder. "Be proud, man. Repeat after me. 'I am a talented artist.'"

He smiled at her and chuckled, but shook his head no.

"Come on. You never hear me apologize for being a genius, do you?" She smirked and wiggled her eyebrows.

"I better go get my zombie shirt on. Bubba is waiting for me with the living dead. His mom is bringing the kids and he has to make sure we don't frighten the little ones." Jackson disappeared behind the doors.

"Sophie, you scared him away," Esther said.

"I scared him? I'm the Good Witch of the North. Everyone loves me." She waved her ruler with a glittery star glued to the end and twirled in the white taffeta dress they had purchased at the thrift store. Glitter from her wand and dress fell everywhere, including on Esther.

Esther brushed the silver sparkles off her witch costume and adjusted her red and white striped tights. "I'm so glad Jackson is staying with the Ironpots."

Sophie straightened her tiara. "Nevaeh loves it at their house too. While she was putting zombie makeup on Parker, I heard her tell Parker that despite the smell of dirty diapers from the other foster kids, it's the happiest home she's ever lived in."

Paisley came out of the cannery dressed as a dead bride holding a bouquet of wilted flowers. "Well, I think we're ready to go. Remember to remind kids not to touch anything and help anyone who gets scared. But I don't think anyone will. It's more like a fun house in there than a haunted house." She shrugged. "Oh, well."

"I love your costume," Esther snickered. "How does Nephi like being your groom?"

"He wanted to be a zombie with Bridget, Parker, and Jackson. But I told him someone had to be my groom."

"He's such a boy," Sophie said.

"Here's how it should go," Paisley said. "Both your dads and Ironpot have the containers for canned food in the parking lot. That will encourage people to donate before they get on the dock. Ms. Priest and your moms are stationed at the baked sale. Everyone will have to walk right past three tables of amazing desserts. Let's hope their kids whine for treats and we sell them all." She grinned and clapped her hands, obviously pleased with her plan.

Paisley pointed at Principal Kelly sitting on a stool by the doors. "He needs to cheer up. What's wrong with him?"

"I think he figured out that Ms. Priest wasn't a fan of his jokes and has the right to file a complaint about his behavior. He's been saying he's sorry a lot lately." Sophie looked at Esther and they snickered.

"Oh, dear," Paisley sighed. "Well, tonight, we've got to cheer him up. He'll hand everyone a bag of popcorn. You will tell the kids they are allowed to throw their popcorn at the spooks, but not to touch anything."

"The popcorn smells delicious. Can we eat some cookies before everyone gets here?" Sophie asked.

"Sure. They are a dollar each." With that Paisley went back into the cannery and Esther could hear her yelling, "Places everyone! It's time to get this show on the road!" A moment later she came back out and marched across the bridge where families were lined up. She moved the sawhorse that had been closing the bridge and had to jog to get across the bridge before kids, chased by parents, caught up to her. She ran past Esther and into the haunted cannery.

An hour later, half the baked goods were gone, but the families were still coming. Esther stopped giving directions for a moment and scanned the crowd. She heard something familiar.

"Girls! Hi!" Madison Merriweather waved at Esther and Sophie from the bridge. Parker's mother, Melissa Stuart navigated the crowd to join Madison and walk with her to the bake sale where Madison stopped to talk to Sophie and Esther.

"Sophie, can you take things for a minute? I want to talk to Madison," Esther said.

"Are you kidding me?" Esther realized Sophie's tiara was crooked and her wand had lost its star and was again, just a ruler.

"I'm sorry, Soph. Just for a minute? Please?"

Sophie blew a hank of hair out of her eyes. "Sure." She pointed the ruler. "Hey, kid! You can throw the popcorn inside. No! Not at Principal Kelly."

Esther pushed through the crowd to Madison. She tapped her on the shoulder.

"Esther," Madison engulfed her in a perfumed hug. "You look adorable."

Esther smiled sheepishly. "Ms. Merriweather? Can I show you something?"

"Of course. Just let me give your mother something first." She dug in her purse and pulled out an envelope. "For the cause." She winked.

"Anything will make a huge difference. Thank you." Esther's mom beamed and put it in the cash box.

"Melissa, do you want to wait here? I'll be right back." Melissa nodded and Madison said, "Okay, my dear. You have my full attention."

"I have something I want you to see." Esther took her arm and led her through the throng to the doors of the cannery.

Madison gasped. "It's the castle in my book. Right down to the last detail. Who did this? This is amazing. I must know." She clasped her hands in delight. "I can't believe it. You must tell me."

"Jackson Green." Esther watched her face for a reaction.

Madison froze for a moment and then looked at Esther. "Isn't that the . . ."

"Yes. But there's more." She turned on her cellphone flashlight and took Madison's hand. "Come inside, just a little way."

With kids flowing around them like water in a river, they entered the haunted cannery. The stone walls didn't stop outside. The entire passageway was painted. There were doors, windows, a coat of arms, and the Bideford family crest from the books. The paintings and portraits looked real. Esther watched Madison reach out to touch one, just as she had before.

"Jackson Green did all this?" Madison's mouth fell open, she stepped back and put a hand over her heart. "Look at that!" She stood stunned. The crowd of running kids and the parents chasing them bumped by. "Where is he?"

"He's here," Esther said loudly over the screams and laughter of the children who had reached the zombies. "Would you like to meet him?"

"I must!"

"If you want to go back outside, I'll bring him to you." Esther smiled. She watched Madison make her way outside, and then went deeper into the maze until she found Jackson.

"Jackson!"

He had his hands up and he was growling at a little boy who was throwing popcorn at him. He couldn't hold the scary face. He broke into laughter as the boy ran out of the room.

"Jackson. Follow me." Esther touched his arm.

"I can't leave."

"They have plenty of undead. I promise you're going to want to come with me." Esther led him outside to Madison who stood behind the bake sale table. She pulled Jackson behind the table and the three of them stepped away from the chaos, closer to the deck railing.

"Jackson, I would like to introduce you to Madison Merriweather."

Jackson's eyes lit up. "I . . . um. You're my favorite author. I'm a huge fan of your books."

Accustomed to her fans, Madison smiled demurely. "And I am a fan of your artwork. Where did you learn to paint like that?"

Jackson shrugged, put his hands in his pockets, and looked down.

"Did you have any formal training?"

He shook his head no and continued looking at his feet.

"Jackson Green, you are one of the most talented artists I have ever come across. You're a genius. I have been wanting to put out a special leather illustrated edition of my first book. Would you be interested in working on it with my publisher?"

Jackson's head snapped up, and he stepped back. He looked at Madison. He made a small smile that exploded into an ear-to-ear grin. "I . . . um . . ."

"Say yes, Jackson." Esther laughed.

"Ah . . . Yes! Yes. Yes." He bounced on his feet.

Madison wrapped his tall frame in her ample hug while he blushed. "Jackson Green, stick with me. We're going to make you enough money for a college degree. You will get a portion of royalties. I am sure we can make this work."

"I don't know." He looked concerned. "I am not very good at school. And my dad will be home from rehab in a few months. I have to help him."

Madison's face softened. "Jackson, my new friend, I have been poor, I have been hungry, and I have taken care of loved ones myself."

Jackson blinked rapidly. "You . . .?"

Madison just nodded. "I know it's hard, but if you're willing, I'm willing to work with you. I see your worth in everything I just witnessed, and in your love and concern for your father."

Esther smiled in satisfaction and left them talking on the dock. Warmth filled her whole body as she walked back to Sophie.

Sophie pointed at her and beckoned her back. She tried unsuccessfully to straighten her disheveled dress. "Don't ever leave me again."

"Never!" Esther hugged her, and straightened her witch's hat, only to get a handful of popcorn thrown in her face. "Peter Ironpot, I am going to get you!"

Halfway through the event, Esther realized Parker was standing next to her. His face was pale, and he had circles under his eyes.

"Parker, you look exhausted." Taking him by the hand, she pulled him to the bake table.

"It's just the zombie makeup. I'm fine." He gave her a tired smile.

"We have tons of zombies. You need a break."

His mother was handing a woman a box of cupcakes when she spotted Esther and Parker. She rushed to his side. "Okay, Parker, you've had enough. Sit down and I'll go find your father."

He plopped into a lawn chair by the cash box and yawned. "I'm not tired. I don't want to go."

Esther knelt down next to him and smiled. "It's been fun, huh? Paisley is an extraordinary event planner."

He chuckled. "After she stops running around like her hair's on fire, things usually go just fine."

"Since we don't have to do the big clean up until the morning, I planned a surprise for everyone. I can give it to you all tonight or tomorrow. Do you want to wait until tomorrow?"

He shook his head. "I don't want to go home."

Esther stood. "What if you and your family go home and you get a solid nap? We should be done here, and you can meet me, Sophie,

Nephi, and Bridget around ten in the garage. If you feel up to it, text me, and let's meet in the garage."

He stood up and put his arms around her. "Tell me."

She shook her head no and laughed.

"I hate surprises. Tell me, please?"

"It's a good surprise."

A smile slowly spread across his face. He sighed. "Okay. But I am not going to sleep until I know what it is."

She gave him a friendly push and stepped back. Trying to make her best mom face, she said, "Sleep! Please. It can wait. You need to get better."

"Parker!" His mom called him from the other side of the table and waved him over. "Let's go. Esther, can you and Nephi give Paisley a ride home?"

Esther nodded. "Sure!"

When he reached his mother, he turned around and called to her. "Esther! See you at ten." His mother put her arm around Parker's waist and they walked back over the bridge to the parking lot.

Chapter Twenty

The Curtain Call

When Esther turned on the garage lights, everything was exactly as she had left it, except Grandma Mable and Mary were in the van.

"Surprise!" Mary leaned out the driver's side window. "Beep, Beep. I can't see! You're blocking my show."

"Grandma. Everyone's going to be here soon."

"Don't worry. We didn't make a mess. But since you dragged my television out here, we didn't have anything to do while you were gone."

"No worries. Can you help me light the fire?"

"Can't you feel it? I lit it about an hour ago. I'll put some more wood in the stove." Grandma Mable climbed out of the van and stoked the fire.

"Did you hear what they found in Angelica's purse?" Esther said.

"Me? No. I've been entertaining short stuff," Mable said.

Esther checked to make sure Mary was fully occupied pretending to drive the van. "We were right. Angelica was planning on using Nevaeh to take the suspicion off of herself. Her plan was to poison Ms. Priest and blame Nevaeh all along. She had a suicide note and the drugs in her handbag. I can't believe she was going to kill her own daughter to protect herself and remove Ms. Priest just to get money from a man."

"Are you sure it was about the money?" Mable asked.

Esther thought while she got a diet soda from the fridge and opened it. "What else would it be about?"

"People who kill multiple people like she has can be thrill-seeking, attention-seeking, crave things I am not going to talk about, or want financial gain," Mable said.

Esther took a sip of the cold drink. "You know, I'm sure we'll find out as it all unravels in court. I also heard that Jackson's father is in a rehab program."

"Well, for Jackson's sake, I hope his journey to recovery is successful." Mable stretched. "Mary, time to get ready for bed." Mary ignored her. Mable turned to Esther and smiled. "So many mysteries to solve and questions to answer in this tiny town. It kind of boggles the mind." She gave Esther a hug and pulled Mary out of the van protesting. "Alright. Now it's not going to be just you and Parker alone, right?"

"Grandma!"

Grandma Mable gave her a probing gaze. "We all intend to be good."

Esther raised her right hand. "I solemnly swear to be good."

"Well, all right. But if you two end up alone out here, you come get me, and Mary can chaperone you." She cackled and took Mary into the house.

Esther checked her invention. She had a table in front of the van with another small table on top of it. She had duct-taped them together. On top of the stack, she had duct-taped Grandma Mable's huge flatscreen television. She'd put an ice chest in the van and filled it with root beer and cream soda. She smiled, pleased with her plan, and opened the garage door all the way. After wiping all traces of Mary from the van, she got the keys out of the ignition and put them in her pocket. Then she turned the lights down and waited.

It wasn't long before the BMW pulled down the driveway. A showered and rested Parker came in with Paisley.

"Surprise!"

"What is this?" His eyes twinkled, and he laughed softly.

"It's a drive-in movie! And that's not all. See? Well, you will. I have a movie for us to watch."

Nephi came in while she was trying to explain her contraption. He patted Parker on the back. "It's a James family tradition. Every year we watch this old black and white movie about a guy that has to spend a night in a haunted house."

Parker tilted his head and raised one eyebrow.

"Trust me. You're going to love it."

Esther opened the driver's door. "Didn't you miss your van? Get in!" She bounced on her feet and smiled from ear to ear."

"I did miss the van. Did you do anything while I was asleep?"

"You're going to love this. Hey. Everyone get in the van." Esther and Parker got in the front. Papa J came quietly into the garage with her mother and watched. Paisley and Sophie sat in the middle seat, Nephi got in the back and stretched his long legs out over the ice chest.

"Okay. Okay." Esther took the keys out of her pocket and shook them until they jingled. "Papa J was out here all day while we decorated the cannery. Go ahead. Turn it over."

He put the keys in the ignition, shifted into neutral, and eyed her warily? "I don't believe it."

She held her breath and crossed her fingers. He turned the key. It sputtered, it popped, and then it rattled and rumbled into life.

"Woo-hoo!" Parker threw his hands in the air and kept yelling. Esther clapped and bounced. Everyone in the car was shouting for joy. Parker pulled her into a quick embrace and then he leapt out of the car and hugged Papa J, smacking him on the back and lifting him up off his feet. Nephi ran around the front of the van and they chest bumped. He kept cheering until he coughed so hard his face turned red.

Paisley slapped him on the back until the fit stopped while Sophie snapped pictures. Nephi picked Sophie up like a baby.

"Put me down, Sasquatch!"

Nephi threw her over his shoulder. "Hart! Get in here. Grace, take a picture."

They gathered into one big pile of friendship and grinned, capturing a moment Esther knew she would always want to remember.

Parker hugged Papa J again and said in a hoarse voice, "Thank you, Bro." He wiped his eyes and kept smiling. "Get in my sweet ride!"

They piled in, and Parker pulled Esther back into another hug. "I can't believe it. I love you! Let's go for a ride!"

"Wait!" Papa J held his hands up. "First, we have to put the wheels back on."

"Right. Right." Grinning from ear to ear, Parker beep, beeped the horn.

White noise woke Esther. The movie was over. The credits were rolling, and someone was snoring softly in the back seat. She was sitting on a cooler in between the front seats so she could be by Parker. She looked around. Everyone was asleep. Nephi's head was against the middle window, mouth open. Paisley was snoring and drooling on his shoulder. Sophie slept in the passenger's seat next to her, leaning against a makeshift pillow.

Parker stirred.

"Sorry. You should go back to sleep."

"No. The movie's over. Mom would worry. What time is it?"

She checked her phone. "Eleven thirty," she said, softly.

It was dark, but she could see his bright smile. "Thank you." He gave her one sweet kiss.

"Gross!" Sophie was awake.

Esther couldn't remember the last time she had felt this happy.

About the Author

© Photo by Haley Miller Captures

Shannon Symonds lives in a small beach town in Oregon where she works, writes, and runs by the sea. She loves her massive extended family, six children, and, well . . . everyone. She is an expert bonfire builder and s'more maker. She believes we can change the world one heart at a time and every small act makes a difference. Her motto is, "Love really is the answer; it always was, and it always will be."

Scan to visit

https://www.cozymysteriesbythesea.com/